Venture Capital Pie

Joe Brink Mystery Book 1

a novel by

Phil Bookman

This is a work of fiction. Names, characters, places, conversations, and incidents are products of the author's imagination or are used fictitiously, and are not to be construed as real.

ISBN-13: 978-1986007597
ISBN-10: 1986007596

Printed in the United States of America

First edition 2018

"There's a cone of silence between two of the pillars over here on our left," the Baron said. "We can talk there without fear of being overheard."

Frank Herbert
Dune

Max: Just a minute, Chief. Isn't this top security?
Chief: Yes.
Max: Well, shouldn't we activate the cone of silence?
Chief: The cone of silence?
Max: Yes.
Chief: Alright, Max. Hodgkins.
Hodgkins: Yes, sir.
Chief: Activate the cone of silence.

Mel Brooks and Buck Henry
Get Smart, "Mr. Big"

A long, long time ago
I can still remember how
that money used to make me smile
And I knew if they heard my pitch
I'd convince them they'd get rich
And maybe they'd be happy for awhile

But the market meltdown made me shiver
With every pitch deck I'd deliver
Bad news on the ticker
I couldn't get much sicker
I remember how hard we tried
To get those VCs to decide
But they just shrugged and we just cried
The day the bubble died

That's when we started singing
Bye, bye venture capital pie
Drove my Prius down to Sand Hill Road
To give it a try
But them good old boys just said
The well had run dry
No more funding for pie in the sky
No more funding for pie in the sky

Prologue

Odysseus Zorba hated Steve Jobs. He figured the man's obsession with thin devices had cost him a few hundred million dollars and set him back ten years.

When Jobs announced the iPhone a decade ago, Dr. Zorba was on the verge of auctioning off his greatest invention to the highest bidder among the world's military and security services. It had passed all the tests with the then current cell phone models. But that damn skinny iPhone had sent Zorba back into the lab, maybe not to square zero, but damn close to it. Good thing he had found Patron, or he would have never recovered.

Too bad Jobs had died. Zorba would have relished killing him with one of his own devices...or what looked like one. Pulling that off would have been tricky, but he was confident that Patron would have found a way.

Ah, well, no sense getting lost in that fantasy. Time to tell Patron the good news. It was time for Odysseus Zorba to cash in on his life's work.

* * *

Dr. Zorba's lab occupied the first two floors of an anonymous, century-old farmhouse on 100 flat acres of chaparral, located between the Pacific Ocean and Santa Cruz Mountains, just west of Santa Clara Valley. His personal quarters were on the third floor. The area was rural, remote and isolated. Zorba worked alone, while the chain-link-fenced property was patrolled 24/7 by armed security personnel and some nasty looking dogs.

Dr. Zorba met Patron in the barn. It looked like an ordinary old barn, was even painted red, but behind the weather-beaten wood facade was a reinforced steel shell clad with sound baffles.

For the next 90 minutes, Dr. Zorba demonstrated several test models. Each worked flawlessly.

Patron punched the air in triumph after each successful test. After the last one was completed, Patron said, "Our potential customers are skeptical. And we can't just give them a sample, the bastards will reverse-engineer it and kiss us off."

Dr. Zorba was unconcerned. He knew Patron already had a plan. Patron always had a plan.

"We need to give them a live demonstration. A vivid one. Here's what I want to do..."

Dr. Zorba loved the plan. It was audacious. It was complicated. It was devious. Perfect!

"I also believe we have some new potential bidders." Patron explained who the newcomers were. "You're going to be rich beyond your wildest dreams."

Dr. Zorba thought Patron underestimated his wildest dreams. Still, he admired Patron's shrewd business mind. Not only would these new bidders push the price up substantially, if they won, they would allow him to extract sweet revenge against the legacy of that dastardly Steve Jobs. Of course, as Patron pointed out, even if they lost, he would get his revenge. Patron's idea was so obvious, he felt stupid that it had not occurred to him before. But, being a self-proclaimed titanic genius, the stupid feeling vanished almost instantly.

Dr. Zorba could not keep the shit-eating grin from wrapping across his face. He would get 50% of the proceeds from the deal, after expenses. He had already selected the luxury condo in Tahiti where he would retire. It was time to work on his French.

It would indeed be a wonderful demo.

Chapter 1
6 months later

And now, from the heart of Silicon Valley, welcome to Venture Capital Pie, *where entrepreneurs pitch for the investments they need to start or grow their companies. But they have to convince our VCs that their idea is worth a slice of the pie, or they'll go home empty-handed.*

Who are our venture capitalists? They're successful Silicon Valley investors and who together have pumped billions of dollars into helping entrepreneurs achieve the American Dream.

Rex Baker is the marketing genius and shrewd investor who has helped turn several tech startups into multi-billion-dollar unicorns.

Doreen Sheehan, senior partner in Sheehan Capital Management, sold the cloud computing company she founded in her kitchen for over five billion dollars.

Bobby Singh came to America as a high school student and used a $10,000 loan to start his IT services company that now employs over 30,000 people.

Dusty Brown started as a secretary in the billion-dollar software company where she is now CEO.

Billionaire Storm Crusher is the former CEO of one of

the world's largest software companies. He's now the hard-charging owner of two major league sports franchises and world-famous Crusher Winery.

* * *

As he waited for the commercial break after the intro to end, Rex Baker, originator and executive producer of *Venture Capital Pie,* took in his surroundings and smiled with satisfaction. The state-of-the-art studio took up an entire floor of an office building on Page Mill Road in Palo Alto. He insisted that his show be broadcast live from the facility he had built-out to his own exacting specifications. The show was so successful that the network acquiesced to this as well as his other often infuriating demands.

Live broadcasting had become a television rarity. Even so-called reality shows used extensive editing to create story flow, building conflict and drama from snippets of digital footage and leaving most of it on the cutting room floor. Going live was considered too risky, but it gave *VC Pie* the gritty, emotional edge viewers loved.

Live meant no time-zone delays. They went on the air at seven o'clock Pacific Time so they could get the all-important ten o'clock Eastern Time audience. Even with almost everyone using a DVR, *VC Pie* was watched live more than any other scheduled primetime show. It was up to Baker to see to it that they kept that unique hold on their audience.

Baker knew he was regarded as a smug, arrogant control freak. This did not at all bother him, since it was true. What others viewed as faults, though, Rex Baker saw as strengths.

After all, he was the one who was rich, famous, and in charge. A small part of him knew that this was rationalization, that he might have been successful despite certain minor flaws in his makeup, not because of them, but it was a very small and increasingly silent part.

VC Pie had not made Baker rich—he was already wealthy when he had started the show—but it had made him famous. That had been what was missing from the life of the lonely little boy who had been too fat, too short and too ungainly to play with the other boys; too nerdy and sloppy to play with the girls. He was still short, but he was now trim, impeccably groomed and dressed, the powerful, debonair man they called Mr. Perfect. Some may not have liked him, but almost everyone sucked up to him.

This included the other VCs sitting with him on stage, all wealthy, successful, extroverted investors, all of whom he detested. They were all seated stage right, in a row of armchairs, with Baker in the middle seat. He had considered having his chair elevated on a platform, like a throne, but decided that wasn't necessary, though he did have his seat padded an extra two inches. It was clear to all that Rex Baker reigned over this domain.

The signal flashed. The commercial break was ending. It was time for the first entrepreneur to pitch. Time for Rex Baker, Mr. Perfect, to focus. Time to go grab some ratings. Show time!

* * *

The announcer intoned, "Our first pitch is for a solution to the problem of private conversations in public places."

The hopeful entrepreneur entered stage left, through large double doors that swung open dramatically. He stopped about 20 feet from the waiting VCs.

"Hello, VCs. My name is David Novak, and I'm looking for an investment of $250,000 for 20% of my company, ShushTek.

"You've all had this problem. You're on your phone, and people around you are overhearing your conversation. Maybe it's something you'd rather keep private. Or maybe you're just annoying them. Or your baby is crying relentlessly on an airplane and the other passengers are ready to kill you both. Well, suffer no more.

"Our product is ShushNik. ShushNik creates a cone of silence, so no one outside its invisible shield can overhear what's said inside. Here, let me give you each a sample."

The twenty-something young man took a tray holding some colorful small devices off a table to his right. Each ShushNik was about the size of a smartphone. He began handing them to the eagerly waiting VCs.

"Gold for Bobby, which I understand is your favorite color."

"It is!"

"Silver for you, Doreen."

"Oh," she said, hefting the device in her hand, "it's so light!"

"Green, the color of money, for Mr. Perfect."

"I love it!" Baker exclaimed, grinning broadly.

"White for you, Dusty."

"Thank you."

He waived the last phone like a matador using his cape to attract a bull. "And red for Storm."

"Watch out," Bobby said in mock alarm, "he may charge at you!"

As Novak resumed his position in front of the VCs, Rex Baker said, "Are you telling me I can talk to Dusty or Doreen without big-ears Crusher eavesdropping?" Baker's feud with Storm Crusher was one of the show's continuing themes.

"You could if you wanted to," Novak said.

"That definitely has my interest. Can we have a demo?"

"You sure can."

As was his center-of-attention habit in such situations, Rex Baker rose from his seat and walked halfway to David Novak. Facing the hopeful supplicant, he said, "Okay, show us how this works."

David held up his black ShushNik, facing the screen outward towards the camera, "You turn it on by pressing the button on the right side, like this." He pressed the button, and the screen lit up.

Each of the VCs looked at their devices, located the button, and pressed it. Then came the explosion.

Chapter 2

Robert B. Parker may have been dead, but other authors had picked up the Spenser series, and I was well into the latest novel featuring my hero and role model when my office phone rang.

Like Spenser's, my office was spartan, a single room on the second floor of an old two-story building on Campbell Avenue, the main street in downtown Campbell, California that housed a frozen yogurt shop and bakery on the first floor. My neighbors along the street side were two Vietnamese financial advisors, Mr. Vu and Mr. Chu, who spent far more time out of the office than in. Across the hall was the Sally Rocket Studio, where my friend Sally Rocket taught self-defense.

I had a desk, desk chair, two guest chairs, and a file cabinet, all bought on sale at Office Depot. I also had a small refrigerator, inherited from a friend who got married and no longer needed it, and a microwave on a counter next to a small sink. There was a flat screen TV on the wall and a laptop computer on my desk. And the phone.

I let the phone ring a second time. No need to appear overanxious.

"Brink Investigations."

"May I please speak to Mr. Brink?" It was a woman's

voice. Already, I was detecting.

"This is Brink." Like Spenser, I just used my last name. Others often insisted on calling me Joe. My mom always called me Joseph.

"My name is Anna Novak. I want to hire you to help my brother."

"Okay. What sort of help?"

"You know the explosion on *Venture Capital Pie?* My brother David is the one they've accused of murdering Rex Baker. He didn't do it, Mr. Brink. We need your help."

I was sorely tempted to do the "pinch self to see if dreaming" thing. This case—we detectives call everything a case—was mega-news. My practice up to then had consisted mainly of getting the goods on errant spouses, along with some insurance and process server work. Would this case be my key to the big time?

* * *

Anna Novak sat down tentatively across from me, on one of my little-used guest chairs. She wore a San Jose State sweatshirt and faded jeans, and her blond hair was pulled back in a ponytail. Her big brown eyes darted around nervously, obviously unimpressed with the humble surroundings. I had the feeling that she might leave at any time.

I knew I wouldn't be helping ease Ms. Novak's concerns, but I had to ask, "How did you come to call me?"

Her expression turned so sad, I thought I might cry. "My brother's public defender made it clear she did not have much of a budget for investigation. We don't have the money for a private lawyer, but we want to do whatever we can for David. I read that you were, um, inexpensive."

I knew what she had read. It had been my 15 minutes of fame. The *San Jose Mercury News* reporter had dubbed me the Accidental Hero and, yes, wrote that my rates were unusually low. Sadly, that had not led to a crush of new business.

I explained my modest fees.

Anna reached into her purse and took out her checkbook. "Our family is not well-off, Mr. Brink. My parents moved to America from Russia when David and I were little. My dad's a handyman, my mom works in a dry cleaner. My brother graduated from Cal Poly where he was a full scholarship student. I'm a senior at San Jose State; I'll graduate this year. My parents invested what little money they had in David's company. But we'll scrape together whatever we can."

Beggars, and detectives with no active cases, cannot be choosers. I took my clean yellow pad, clicked my pen, and jotted down some notes, the beginnings of a case file. Detective rule number one, write everything down. Only a fool trusts his memory for the many details that make up a case.

"Ms. Novak, I saw the explosion, along with millions of others. It seems pretty clear that your brother gave Rex Baker the device that killed him."

She shook her head, looking even sadder, if that was possible. "I was watching as well. But David says he has no idea how it exploded. So, you need to find out what really happened."

I got some more basic information: full names, addresses, email addresses, phone numbers, and so forth. Wrote it all down. Took her check for my retainer. Anna Novak had nothing else useful to tell me. I shook her soft, slim hand, told her I'd go see her brother, and sent her on her way.

* * *

Sylvia Sanchez was David Novak's public defender. She told me over the phone that she had a huge caseload, and the expectation was that she would try to cut the best deal she could for her client. No one in government, she said, wanted to bear the cost of a trial for what appeared to be an open-and-shut case.

Except, perhaps, for the District Attorney. This was an unusually high-profile case, and the DA was a rabid publicity hound. The national press had instantly dubbed the death of Rex Baker as the Perfect Murder, and the meme had gone viral. I was certain that the DA's idea of the best possible deal idea might not be one that was kind to my new client.

Sylvia said she would certainly work with me so long as the county wasn't paying, but her lack of enthusiasm was evident. I got her to agree to share all discovery with me, and to get me on David's visitor's list at the county jail right away.

Chapter 3

I drove to the main jail on Hedding Street in my second-hand Prius. I could barely afford the payments, but it used virtually no gas and made me feel at one with Silicon Valley. I was going to get red, which was sort of the default color in the Valley, but remembered that detectives were not supposed to stand out. So, I had gone for subtle, dark gray. It was also the cheapest one on the dealer's lot the day I went shopping.

I met David Novak in a room used mainly for client visits by attorneys. We sat across from each other at a small table that was bolted to the floor. David wore an orange jumpsuit, his hands were cuffed in front, and the guard who brought him in refused to remove them. The guard waited outside, watching us through a window in the door.

David was tall and lean, all angles and planes. Even after spending several days in jail, he had the arrogant, condescending demeanor that seemed characteristic of many Russian men. I reminded myself that my view of this may have been through some sort of American distortion field, coupled with my limited experience with Russian guys, mainly a couple of college assholes whose oligarch fathers were paying their way to an American education. And, anyway, David had grown up in California, not Russia.

David slouched down in his seat and looked at me incredulously. *"You're* my detective?"

On the other hand, maybe it was not just a stereotype. "My name is Brink. I'm a private investigator. I've been hired by your family to assist in your defense."

"Brink what?"

"Just Brink will do."

"Whatever. How old are you?" he said, as if suppressing a laugh.

About the same as you. But I'm not in jail for murder. "You've been charged with murder, Mr. Novak. It would be helpful if you let *me* ask the questions before we run out of time here. Unless you want me to leave."

His expression changed on a dime. Duly abashed, he shook his head rapidly, sat up straighter. "No, no, look, I'm sorry. Please, ask your questions."

The rule of jail visits is that you only get a small timeslot, and the guards always find an excuse to end it early. It does no good to protest; they have all the power. So, I got right to it.

I quickly explained to David that attorney-client privilege extended to me. I had gotten Sylvia to agree to have me as part of the official defense team, which meant that whatever David told me was privileged communication.

David ("Please don't call me Dave") had graduated from Cal Poly. He worked for Google for a few of years, left for a startup which failed, then started ShushTek with a friend. He was CEO and a 50-50 partner.

He wanted to tell me about how a ShushNik worked, but I cut him off. *Maybe some other time,* I thought, but I needed to focus on some very specific matters, and I was mindful of time passing.

The devices he had handed out on *VC Pie* were prototypes, he said, in response to my first question. They were made by a Chinese outfit that specializes in device prototyping. I had him walk me through the process, from ordering the units used in the show until the time he passed them out. I wanted to pin down as well as possible where those gadgets were and when, who had access to them, and who could have either tampered with the green one or switched it.

I asked him for a quick history of his company, not hard to do for a year-old old startup. I also got some basic information about his partner.

We discussed how David had gotten onto *Venture Capital Pie,* and who he had dealt with in the process. He swore he had never met any of the show's VCs before he walked out on the set that night, and had no animosity towards Rex Baker or any of the rest of them.

I was done with my questions and was about to tell the guard we were through, when something occurred to me. "You were, what, ten feet from Rex Baker when the thing exploded?"

"About that, yes."

"How come you weren't hurt?"

"Oh, I was hurt all right, it just doesn't show. I got blown off me feet and on my ass. I was out cold for a few minutes. I have a mild concussion and hurt like hell all over. The doc said the shock wave messes up your insides, and the only thing to do is rest and let them heal." He looked around and snorted sardonically. "So, I'm in here, resting and healing."

The last thing David said to me, before the guard came in and announced that time was up, was, "Listen, Brink, I wanted their money. None of them had turned me down yet, so I still loved all of them."

The one question I knew not to ask, though I had to restrain myself, was, "Did you do it?" I was part of David's defense team, and had watched enough detective and courtroom dramas on TV to know it was best for the defense not to know, if only so that you avoided suborning perjury should you need your client to testify on his own behalf. In other words, if a defense attorney knew the defendant was guilty, she could not let him go on the witness stand and say he was innocent. If she did not know for sure, well...

* * *

David Novak was right, I was young to be a private investigator.

I had graduated from college with a major in miscellaneous bullshit just as the Great Recession was plunging the tech sector in Silicon Valley into a deep slump. While the warm body principle made miscellaneous bullshit a desirable degree when the Valley was booming, it had been worthless when yours truly entered the workforce.

Fortunately, I had also minored in trying to get laid. A girlfriend introduced me to her uncle, who just happened to be looking for warm, cheap bodies to hire. The relationship with the girl did not last, but the job did.

Curt Kowalski was the uncle. He had retired from the Santa Clara County Detective Bureau, worked in the private sector, then started Kowalski-Wu Investigations with Amy Wu. It seems that crime goes up when the economy goes down, and that includes the kind of white-collar crime that

Kowalski-Wu specialized in. So, they were hiring a few gofers—they called us apprentices. It was a job requiring few skills beside reliability, along with reasonably good health and a willingness to learn and work hard. That was me.

I spent four years working my ass off and acquiring all sorts of odd skills. Along the way, I qualified to take the state private investigator exam. When I passed, Curt offered to give me a promotion and a nice raise.

I sincerely thanked him, but I had other ideas.

I had a choice to make. I could take Curt's offer and finally move out of my parents' house and get my own place. Or I could go into business for myself. Silicon Valley's stratospheric real estate and rental prices would not let me do both.

During my apprenticeship, I had become an avid reader of private eye novels. My two favorite heroes were Spenser and Elvis Cole. Each worked for himself out of a small, rundown office. I decided that's what I would do, though the small, rundown part would be out of necessity, not a desire for hardboiled grit.

But it wasn't hero worship that got me to go out on my own. I had learned a great deal about myself since graduating college, and one of the major lessons was that I hated having a boss. Not that Amy Wu or Curt Kowalski were bad bosses. They were both demanding, but not unreasonably so, and had taken a kid who was still wet behind the ears and turned him into a real PI, albeit still a green one. I not only learned the PI business from them, I sort of grew up under their watch.

But I had also seen my father chafe every day at his management, and he still had decades of kowtowing ahead of him. It was not what I wanted for myself.

Growing up, I had always liked being in charge, and, even though I had not yet figured out how to consistently get others in a group let me lead, I wanted to at least be in charge of myself. In fact, it felt like more than a want. I badly needed my autonomy. What better time to go for it than when I had so little to lose, so few responsibilities? Though I got the irony that getting my so-called autonomy also meant living with my parents for who knew how much longer.

Chapter 4

I stopped at the Public Defender's office, which is not far from the main jail. Sylvia Sanchez had called to tell me she had the first batch of discovery documents she had received from the DA's office. Visitor parking was full, so I ended up parking two block away and walking.

Sylvia was fortyish, with streaks of gray in her black hair. She greeted me with a wry grin and extended hand. "Welcome to the David Novak defense team."

I shook her hand. Nice and firm. "Thanks."

"I've just been informed that the DA is offering no deals, at least not yet. We're heading to trial. Murder one. I've also been told by the powers that be that we need to demonstrate that we're vigorously defending our client, so having the Accidental Hero on our team is a good thing. Welcome aboard." Her grin was no longer wry; she was mocking me. At least she didn't roll her eyes.

* * *

California is a no-fault divorce, community property state. You don't need grounds to get a divorce, or evidence of bad behavior to get more of your spouse's money when you split. Yet a great deal of PI business is getting evidence of spousal infidelity. I don't get it. If you distrust your spouse so much that you're willing to pay a PI to try to catch them cheating, why stay married to them? I've been told this is my youthful, never-been-married naiveté showing.

Of course, there are those with prenups who have a lot at stake if they can prove infidelity. But those folks are in far different tax brackets than my clientele.

Regardless, Kowalski-Wu did not deign to handle such business. If it came their way, they referred it out. Fortunately for me, they had been tossing enough of that my way, along with other small jobs, to keep me afloat.

Which is how I became the Accidental Hero.

* * *

I was staking out one of the no-tell motels along El Camino Real in Santa Clara, the kind where the rooms open right onto the parking lot. My client was referred by Kowalski-Wu. I had followed his wife from her home in Los Altos to a rendezvous with her boyfriend, and had snapped pictures of them when he opened the door to room 22 to let her in. My trusty Nikon DSLR camera with its telephoto lens was one of my most important pieces of investigative gear.

I was parked on the street with a clear view of room 22. It would have been too conspicuous to sit in the motel parking lot while I waited for the lovebirds to leave and give me my parting closeups. A good deal of PI work is waiting.

It was getting dark. I needed to keep watch and avoid the temptation to fiddle with my phone. To avoid dozing off, I was naming the capitals of all 50 states, but was struggling with South Dakota, when a knock at my window startled me.

I opened the driver's side window, coming face to face with a pair of big brown eyes. The girl looked to be about seven years old. She was holding hands with a little boy who might have been three or four and was sucking his thumb. The kids were dressed in jeans and T-shirts, barefoot, and it was a chilly evening.

"Mister, can you help us?"

"Sure. What's wrong?"

"We need to go home."

"Where's home?"

She shrugged.

"Where are your parents?"

"My mom doesn't know where we are."

"How did you get here?"

"He took us."

"Who took you?"

Her eyes got wide and she ducked down, pulling the boy with her. I looked out the passenger window to my right, in the direction she'd been looking. Charging across the motel lot was a snarling, barefoot man in a wife-beater and black jeans. He bellowed something unintelligible. He was heading right for us.

I opened the driver's side door, got out, tossed the kids inside, shut the door and locked it just as the raging bull reached the passenger side. He tried that door, and I thought he might actually rip it off when he found it was locked. He bashed at the window with his fist. The window won.

Shaking his hand in pain, he came around the front of the car. He raised his sore fist, the one he'd tried to use to smash the window, and was about to deck me when I stepped to my left, swung the weapon I was holding in my right hand up, and clobbered him in the jaw. He staggered, and I brought my weapon down on top of his head. Twice. He wasn't unconscious, but close enough. I used my belt to tie his hands behind him and called 9-1-1.

* * *

The kids were Sofia and Diego Ramirez. Sofia said they had been kidnapped by their mother's ex-boyfriend while mom was at work cleaning houses, and had been gone three days. When Jesus Varga fell asleep, Sofia unlocked the door and the kids made their break.

They had been living on delivered pizza, soda and beer. Jesus had hit them a few times the first day until they got the message and stayed quiet and compliant. But they were physically okay.

I was just finished giving my statement to detectives at the police station when Isidora Ramirez was reunited with her children. I walked over and Sofia introduced me to her mom. I gave Isidora my business card and told her to call me if she ever needed help. Sofia asked me for a card, too, which I gave her, repeating what I'd told her mom.

The kidnapping had gotten some press coverage, and there were photographers and reporters on hand to witness the happy ending. I somehow got pulled into a somewhat staged, tearful group hug with mom and the kids, which made a great front-page photo and local TV news lead-in on a slow news day.

Of course, I was interviewed. I tried to duck out, but got

cornered by a gaggle of reporters. I only said a few sentences, but they were enough. The story of a young private eye who happened to be nearby on another mysterious case, one he would not talk about, bravely rescuing these two adorable waifs, was irresistible.

And then there was that unfortunate quote. One of the reporters asked me how it felt to be a hero. "If I'm a hero, it was an accident," I said.

Thus was born the Accidental Hero. The Internet ate it up for a day.

I know I did not say anything about being inexpensive, but that somehow got into the *San Jose Mercury News* story. In any case, until Anna Novak walked into my office, the publicity had not brought me much business, but did garner a few crank calls and a lot of teasing from friends and random strangers.

The bigger impact was that I had lost an expensive camera; Jesus Varga's skull had done it in. It had been the only weapon handy. At least I managed to recover the great photos I had taken for my client, and kept his name out of the information I gave to the cops.

Chapter 5

Sylvia escorted me into her tiny office. There were stacks of case files everywhere, on her desk, her two guest chairs, and the floor.

She swept the office with her hand. "The good news is that most of these cases are being reassigned. This is one of the highest profile cases the Public Defender's office has handled in some time, so I get to stop dealing with the meat market for a while."

The meat market was the daily criminal court arraignment of cases, most of which were plea-bargained in just a few minutes time. Typically, the attorney, usual a PD, met the client for the first time, chatted with an assistant DA, told the client what they risked by going to trial, got buyoff on a plea deal, and the two lawyers presented the judge with their agreement. It's wholesale, assembly-line justice, but without it, the court system would become completely constipated and hopelessly costly.

Sylvia relocated a pile of files from one chair to an open spot on the floor, and I sat down. I was coming in late to the party. David had already been arraigned, charged with first degree murder, and denied bail. Sylvia said that the arraignment, during which the prosecution must make a case to the judge for probable cause, had not revealed much about the prosecution's case. The judge had seen the murder take place live on TV. The assistant DA had not needed to present too much evidence to get to probable cause.

Together, we reviewed the discovery.

The lab had determined that the bomb employed some type of plastic explosive, the kind used by the military and intelligence services, as well as terrorists. I later found out online that plastic explosives were also used commercially. There were tight inventory control requirements, but the amount in the smartphone-sized device was so small that trying to track its source would be next to impossible.

The lab report stated that the detonator was destroyed in the blast, but there were a variety of tiny ones that were readily available and would have been easily coupled to the device's battery and on-off button.

I got the sense that assembling the bomb itself would not have been difficult. The tricky part was putting it in a ShushNik case and closing it so it looked right. The whole thing was not rocket science, but it took some skill. Of course, as with all explosive devices, you couldn't test it, so whoever did this had to get it right the first time.

The other useful material in the discovery were transcripts of detective interviews with David's partner, Hudson Ambrose. They confirmed what David had told me about where the devices had been and who had access to them.

The five colored ShushNiks given to the VCs during the show had been one-offs. All the other prototypes were black. All five had been tested by Hudson and David, together, the day before the show. The devices had all worked fine. They were left on the table David used as a desk overnight, plugged into a power strip, topping off their batteries, in the living room of the one-bedroom apartment that served as ShushTek's office and where David resided.

In the morning, the devices remained where they had been left the night before. The partners rehearsed and refined David's pitch. After a lunch in the office of peanut butter and jelly sandwiches, they gave the ShushNiks another on-off test, just to be sure they powered up. They then did another run-through of the pitch, with Hudson taking a video that they watched together and critiqued. At about four o'clock, David put the devices, along with a couple of the standard black prototypes, into an attaché case, and they drove separately to the studio.

At the studio, David, in Hudson's presence and accompanied by an assistant producer, removed the five devices from his attaché case and placed them on a tray on a table on the set. David and Hudson gave each device a final on-off test, then the assistant producer arranged them and the tray for the proper camera angle. They then left the stage. Since ShushTek was up first, that was where they assumed the devices had stayed, though neither Hudson nor David had seen them again until the show began.

We had our window. Unless both Hudson and David were lying, which was unlikely since the assistant producer could confirm that last on-off test, sometime between the time those devices went on the table at about 5 p.m. and the start of the show at 7 p.m., the green device had been changed out for the bomb.

We discussed the discovery material. Sylvia agreed that we needed to show that someone else could have swapped the green device for the bomb during that two-hour window, when there were probably lots of people milling around.

"That might give us reasonable doubt," she said, "but it's thin. It would be better if we could point to a specific alternative suspect."

"Why did they arrest David and not Hudson? From what's in the discovery, it seems just as likely that they did it together as that David did it on his own."

"My question precisely. They went easy on Hudson in their interview. It makes me think they have other evidence we haven't seen yet."

"Can they do that?"

"The prosecution has to provide evidence under discovery in a reasonable amount of time. They're not supposed to sandbag evidence. But there are any number of ways they can delay labelling something officially as evidence. Like, they can say they were pinning it down or hadn't yet conducted an official interview, that sort of thing. Which is why I'm interviewing Hudson Ambrose tomorrow. Want to join me?""

"Yes."

We discussed next steps, or, more accurately, my next steps. I soon had a long list, and said so.

"Oh, it'll get longer. We have a murder trial scheduled in six months. We've barely begun."

Chapter 6

No sooner did the news get out that the Accidental Hero was part of the David Novak defense team, then the Internet trolls started in. What was Novak doing with a private investigator if he was so poor he needed a public defender? Outrage!

Overnight, I had gone from being an asset to a political liability. Never mind that David easily qualified for a public defender. He'd had no income for a year, used up his savings and maxed out his credit cards. His partner was paying for his apartment and he drove a ten-year-old clunker. That his family could scrape together a few bucks to pay my shamefully low rates was irrelevant. Except in the court of public opinion.

The Santa Clara County Public Defender's office had over a hundred lawyers and paralegals, along with 30 or so investigators. I was worried that the Public Defender, a county employee, might bow to political pressure and toss me off the case. I wondered why I cared so much. The Novak family was paying me peanuts, so it wasn't the money.

I told all this to Sally Rocket. We were eating breakfast at a pancake house near my office. You can't walk ten steps in downtown Campbell without being in front of some sort of eatery.

Every private eye needs a trusty sidekick. They also should be brutish and enigmatic. Spenser had Hawk. Elvis Cole had Joe Pike. I had Sally Rocket.

Trusty, definitely. I had already trusted Sally with my life, and, if I had to do it again, she would be my first choice.

Brutish, not really. Hawk and Pike are physically intimidating characters. Their very appearance strikes fear into the hearts of the toughest bad guys. Sally may have been slightly stocky, but she was still a five-foot-five young woman. Not your typical scary thug. However, she was a tough, skilled, even vicious fighter. And she had definitely mastered the black ghetto stare. When she made her hard-ass, mess-with-me-at-your-peril face, it even gave me a chill.

As for enigmatic, Sally's background was a closed book. She simply would not go there. It's as if she had not existed before we met. She's equally tight-lipped about her personal life. Yet I feel we are open and intimate with each other. It's just that, while I am an open book, she has these boundaries I sometimes run into.

"Maybe I should just bow out," I said through a mouthful of pancakes.

"But you don't want to," Sally said.

"Who needs the headaches? I'm not making much anyway, and they're gonna run out of money long before this is over."

"You need to do this case."

"Why?"

"Because you're a hero and there's another damsel in distress."

"Anna Novak?"

"Just like Sofia Ramirez. I bet she has big eyes."

That she does. "You think I have a hero complex?"

"I think you don't want to back out on your commitment to a fair maiden. And this case could erase the accidental label."

It would be nice to be just a plain old hero. "Okay, I'll keep the case. But how?"

"Do something heroic." Sally speared a sausage and popped it into her mouth.

* * *

I met Sylvia in the lobby of the Public Defender's building for our interview with Hudson Ambrose. Knowing the parking situation, I had wisely given myself extra time.

"I'm going to do this case pro bono," I said, before she had a chance to tell me to take a hike. This was Sally's heroic suggestion.

When I went to work for Kowalski-Wu, it had taken me a while to figure out that "pro bono" had nothing to do with being in favor of Bono. Shows how self-absorbed I was in my collegiate pursuit of miscellaneous bullshit. Now, I liked it better than saying "free"—the Latin sounded so professional.

"Well, shut-up! That should silence the trolls and my politically sensitive bosses. The Accidental Hero strikes again!"

Hudson Ambrose was waiting for us in the tiny interview room. We sat in plastic chairs at a small table. He looked to be in his late twenties and seemed relaxed.

Sylvia introduced me to Hudson. I was just "Joe Brink, the investigator on the case."

"We need to ask you some questions in order to help David," Sylvia said.

"Sure, anything."

We had agreed that Sylvia would ask the questions until we got to the day of the TV show. To make Hudson comfortable, she started with some softballs. Full name, age, address, school and work history. All easy stuff. Then she got down to business.

"How did you and David start ShushTek?"

"We've known each other since college. David was talking about doing a startup. I was getting bored at my company, we had this cool idea, so I said, 'What the hell?'"

"How did you fund the company?"

"In bits and pieces. We're equal partners. David is CEO and I'm CTO. At first, we both put in money as we needed it. I live at home and my folks are well off, and I have some savings. David was pretty broke because he hadn't gotten paid for a couple of months before his old company went bust. He got some money from his parents, who don't have much, and I've been paying for things the last few months. Which is cool. We also did a Kickstarter campaign that finished just before the TV show."

"How did that go?"

"Great. We went for 20k. We got 108k. Next, we needed to close an A round to fund initial production. So much for that now. Thing is, I don't know exactly what to do. I'm in way over my head."

"No other investors?"

"No, we own all the stock. We decided to take a crack at *VC Pie* before going out to other VCs for our A round. It was something David really wanted to try, he said the PR would be great even if we didn't get a slice. He also had something to prove."

"What was that?"

"Well, it was Rex Baker who forced the startup he was working for out of business. He was hoping Rex would make an offer so he could turn him down."

Our faces must have given our surprise away, because Hudson looked back and forth from one of us to the other a few times. "Didn't David tell you that?"

Now we know why they only charged David, I wrote on my yellow pad and showed it to Sylvia. She glanced at it and nodded.

Sylvia pumped Hudson for details about what had happened at David's former company, and we both took a lot of notes. He said David had been bitter and a bit obsessed about what had gone down, and had talked a lot about it.

Then it was my turn. I took Hudson through the day of the TV show in minute detail. I got nothing that contradicted what David had said.

After about another hour, we thanked Hudson and sent him on his way. Then we headed to a nearby burger place. We both agreed that we needed cheeseburgers and fries to help us debrief.

David's former outfit had been a typical VC funded startup. Baker's VC firm, Rex Baker Venture Partners, had the ability to get its money out if the startup failed to meet certain milestones within two years. The company failed to make the grade, and Rex Baker Venture Partners chose to liquidate the business. They did not get their money back, but they did wring out every drop of cash there was to get, right down to selling the office furniture and equipment.

Employees and creditors were left in the lurch, told to feel free to sue.

David had not been a part of the founding team, but he had been brought in by one of the founders, his former boss and mentor at Google. The man committed suicide weeks after the startup folded.

Sylvia plucked a fry, examined it, nodded, and said, “They have the prosecution’s holy grail, motive. It lets them tie up the evidence into a simple narrative for the jury. David wanted revenge and chose to get it in a most public way. Case closed.”

“Not what he told me.” I told her his “I still loved them all” line.

“Not what he told me, either. But clients always lie.”

“Don’t they know about attorney-client privilege?”

“It’s the first thing I explain. Doesn’t matter. They always manage to find something to lie about.”

I shook my head. I had not worked directly with a defense attorney before.

“Don’t be so surprised. My clients are usually guilty. Most are varying degrees of sociopath and lying is second nature to them. Maybe first nature. Anyway, I’m a government employee, which make them trust me even less than they would otherwise.”

“We need to talk to him about this.”

“I’ll talk to him,” she said. “As you pointed out, Joe Brink, you have a lot of investigating to do.”

When I got in my car, I looked up two things on my phone. I had not wanted to appear to Sylvia to be a complete rube. A few minutes later, I knew that a CTO was chief technology officer, and that an A round was the first in what are usually a series of rounds of venture capital funding for a startup.

* * *

Dargo was standing on the pedestrian bridge over San Tomas Expressway where the busy highway sliced through Campbell. It was a great place to have a private phone conversation. He could see both ends of the bridge, and it was mainly used by kids going to and from John D. Morgan Park from the tract homes on the other side of the road. He had been nosing around Campbell getting the lowdown on Joe Brink. Now he was reporting in.

"I'm telling you, Boss, it's in the bag."

"Better be. No room for mistakes."

"I got it covered. They charged the right guy. Only took a little nudge to be sure of that. He's got a career public defender, poor bastard. And now, he's got this Accidental Hero greenhorn investigator, who, I am told, could not detect his own ass with both hands and a map."

"Whatever it takes. Just be sure everything goes as planned."

Dargo tossed his burner phone off the bridge. It bounced twice before an 18-wheeler pancaked it.

Chapter 7

Everyone who works on a TV show seems to be some flavor of producer.

Okay, not the actors and stage hands and cameramen and such, but still, there are lots of producers. In addition to plain old producers and co-producers, there are executive producers, co-executive producers, consulting producers, supervising producers, coordinating producers, associate producers, assistant producers, and on and on. What I learned from the pretty receptionist at the Rex Baker Studio was that if you knew someone was a producer, you did not know anything useful. You had to ask what they actually did. So, I told her the type of person I needed to see, and why. Then I took a seat and cooled my heels for a half hour.

The receptionist finally rescued me from phone-fiddling and directed me to the set, which she informed me in a hushed voice was no longer a crime scene. The set was bare, stripped of furniture. There was some minor damage from the bomb in the center of the floor, but not much. If I did not know what had happened there, I wouldn't have even noticed it.

Waiting for me with her arms folded was associate producer Becky Tahara. She was the day-to-day manager of the show. I handed her my card. It read Brink Investigations; no name, just a phone number and address.

"My name's Brink. I'm the investigator on the David Novak case."

We shook hands. Her handshake was firm but brief.

"You work for the defense, right?"

Did I forget to mention that? "I do." I looked around as if in awe. "So, this is where they do the show."

She looked at me impassively, hands on slender hips, not responding to my feigned wonderment. "How can I help you, Mr. Brink?"

"Can you tell me what happens to the show now?"

"That just got resolved this morning and will probably hit the evening news. The network had right of first refusal in case of Mr. Baker's death. They decided to exercise that right."

"Which means?"

"Which means the network is buying the show from Rex Baker Studios and will continue it. Details to follow."

"So, you all have jobs?"

"That I don't know. My bet is they move production to L.A. or New York. Some of us will probably be offered jobs there."

She folded her arms and stared at me imperiously. Time to cut to the chase. I asked her who had access to the Shush-Niks while they were on the table between 5 and 7 p.m. on the day of the show.

Becky paused and seemed to be counting in her head. "I'd say about 20 people." She pointed. "The table was right there, out in the open, and there were lots of staff milling around, doing all sorts of things, pretty much that whole time."

"I need a list of them."

"I need a subpoena."

Thanks for the help. I had served numerous subpoenas and knew what they were, and Sylvia said she could usually get them, but preferred not to if possible. Something about saving them for the really big things, that judges did not like repeated defense requests for subpoenas for a case because the prosecution invariably pleaded harassment or fishing expedition. I flashed my most charming smile. "I can get one, but can't you help me out here."

"Then get one. You're working for the guy who murdered my boss in front of 10.25 million viewers. You should be glad I'm talking to you at all."

She knew exactly how many people had been watching. I wondered what was more important to her, the death of her boss or the ratings. Then I remembered something Sylvia had told me. "Well, okay, then maybe I'll just have the defense attorney schedule a deposition." Sylvia had said that a deposition sounded intimidating to most people and usually loosened them up, especially if they had never been deposed before.

"I'll see you then." Becky turned on her heel and walked away. I guess she was immune to intimidation and my boyish charm.

I made my way back to the reception desk and asked for the assistant producer, whose role the helpful receptionist had earlier explained to me. After another wait, a gorgeous young woman came up to me and introduced herself as Misty Morning. My finely tuned detecting skills were hard at work. I had already deduced that Rex Baker liked beautiful women, because Misty was the third woman I had met at the Rex Baker Studio, and they were all beautiful.

I gave her my card and introduced myself. Misty was the most stunning of the three, and I was falling in love. She must have misinterpreted my expression, because she said, "Yes, that's really my name. My father was a prankster and my mom was sweet and loving, but, like, spacey?"

She said it like a question, but I didn't think I was supposed to answer. I adjusted what I realized was a dopey look on my face. "What exactly do you do here?" I wanted to confirm what the receptionist had told me.

"My job is selecting the companies to come on the show and then working with them?"

Misty had the Valley Girl speech pattern of making statements sound like questions. I usually found that annoying, but with her, it seemed endearing. We walked down a hall and into Misty's office. We sat down, Misty behind her desk, me across from her.

As much as Becky had attitude, Misty was bubbly and forthcoming. She walked me through the process, from the time a company applied, through the screening process, until the day they appeared on the show if selected.

"How did it go for ShushTek?"

"Great. It usually takes, like, six months to get on the show, but they did it in three? I remember that because it was so unusual."

"How did they do that?"

"David and Hudson were always, like, completely prepared and did everything promptly. Like they knew just what we wanted?"

A sudden dark cloud marred Misty's delicate face. "It was horrible, Mr. Brink."

"Please, call me Joe." Misty calling me "mister" made me think I should re-evaluate this last name only thing. Part of why I did it was to seem more mature. But now I just felt old, at least as compared to Misty. *I wonder how old she is?*

She scrunched her perfect eyebrows as if I had said something odd. "I blame myself."

"How could you be to blame?"

"Just because you're good at the process doesn't mean you should be on the show. It's mainly about entertainment value and balance." She sounded like she was repeating memorized lines.

I gave her my "tell me more" nod.

"We know what kind of products and presenters add share, and which reduce it."

"What's share?"

"It's a show's share of viewers? Each point of share is about 1.2 million viewers?"

I was getting used to her statement-as-a-question routine.

"So, it's like ratings?"

"The same thing, really. Anyway, even though we're all about Silicon Valley and VCs, we only have one tech product on each show. People often have trouble relating to tech, but, like, they love food products. We have product categories and a rating system we use to rank the audience value of a particular product."

"Interesting." I noticed she had dropped the question inflection.

"They also need to relate to the presenter. Techies are often either too good at pitching, all numbers and funding jargon, or they're too geeky, or both. The audience likes a mixture of down-to-earth people like themselves and goobers they can feel superior to, with the occasional really polished presenter thrown in. Kids and moms and people with interesting personal stories score highest. We have a system for rating that, too."

"Sounds complicated."

She bit her lower lip. So cute! "It is. Like I said, it's all about balance, getting the right mix on each show."

"Who makes those decisions?"

"A group of us. We have a weekly meeting, I present applicants ready for a decision and we slot the ones we pick into upcoming shows."

"Was Mr. Baker part of the selection committee?"

"Just him, Becky and me. Mr. Baker was very particular. He made all the final decisions. That's the thing."

"What thing?"

"He wasn't sure about ShushTek. I think he could have gone either way. But Becky and I sort of tipped it. We thought the idea of a cone of silence would be fun. Mr. Baker said it made him think of *Get Smart,* a really old TV show I had to look up." She wiped a tear that had leaked out of her left eye. "I remember, he said, 'What's next, a shoe phone?' Anyway, Becky pushed real hard and he finally went along with it. The thing is, if I had said no, maybe Mr. Baker would have agreed with me. Then none of this would have happened."

I asked about who had access to the set during the 5 p.m. to 7 p.m. timeslot. She told me that she had, just moments ago, been told not to give me that information. Becky must have spoken to her as soon as she left me.

"I may have said too much already," Misty said, again

scrunching her brow.

Other than confirming David and Hudson's story about the last on-off test at about 5 p.m., Misty seemed to have nothing else useful she could tell me about that day. She was off the set after that and had not noticed anything unusual.

"If you think of anything else, no matter how insignificant, call me," I said, trying to sound encouraging but not too needy.

"I will."

"It wasn't your fault," I said as I left her in reception. I wanted to hug her. I managed to retain my professional demeanor. But she sure had big eyes.

Chapter 8

You always investigate the victim. Everyone knew that from watching cop shows on TV. I, a licensed private eye, knew that from my training. Also, Sylvia Sanchez had put it near the top of my list.

Sylvia had already approved getting a thorough backgrounder on Rex Baker. There's this online service called DeepDig that does them. In addition to pulling together everything online, about a person, often including things in so-called secure databases, there's an actual human who assembles and curates the report. It's too expensive for casual use, but they do a first-class job. Sylvia made it a point of telling me that I had to use DeepDig sparingly because of the cost. "Only with my explicit approval."

The bottom line was that Rex Baker was a tough, shrewd marketing guy who had clawed his way up from a middle-class family to become a consultant to some of the top tech companies in Silicon Valley, just as the Internet was taking off. He started his own VC firm, Rex Baker Venture Partners, right after the dot-com bust, and built a fortune backing some of the new generation of Valley giants in their infancy. His net worth was estimated by DeepDig to be $500 million.

Along the way, he had made a lot of enemies. He'd been

sued so many times that a Palo Alto law firm was said to have a wing named after him. Charming and polished, but ruthless and arrogant was the consensus description of Rex Baker.

* * *

It's always tricky for the defense to interview the victim's family and friends. They usually refuse to talk to you or are hostile, sometimes aggressively so. Which is why I was pleasantly surprised when Ryan Baker readily agreed to meet with me.

After leaving Misty, I went out to the parking lot and grabbed lunch from a taco truck that should have been called a burrito truck. Then I drove up 280 to the Baker estate in Atherton, where the average home price was over $10 million. The Baker abode definitely pulled that average up. There was an actual guard at the gate, who took my ID and vetted me over the phone. I then drove for several hundred yards along a brick driveway to the front portico, where I was met by another serious guy in a dark suit. He escorted me through what looked like the lobby of a five-star Hawaii resort, to an equally impressive pool area, where I was greeted politely by my host.

Rex Baker's son looked nothing like his father. Ryan was a good foot taller than his dad, about six-four, tan and athletic, with a full head of hair. Rex may have reached the stage of life where impeccable grooming and self-assurance made a man distinguished looking; Ryan was just plain leading-man handsome.

So far, Sylvia had refused to spring for DeepDig for anyone except Rex Baker, so I had to do my research through what was freely available online. There was surprisingly little information about Ryan Baker. I knew he was 25 years old and had a bachelor's degree from the University of Hawaii.

"Good to meet you, Mr. Brink. I just finished a round of golf and was thinking about a drink. Can I get you something?"

It was mid-afternoon, the day was warm and sunny, and we were seated under an umbrella at a patio table next to a large, crystal-clear pool, surrounded by palm trees. *Where do I check in?* "How about a Piña Colada?"

Ryan smiled as if it was the most brilliant idea he had ever heard. "Great idea! Christopher, would you fetch us a couple of Piña Coladas?"

The man who had escorted me in disappeared in search of our drinks.

"How can I help you, Mr. Brink?"

"You understand that I'm part of David Novak's defense team?" I was careful to be up front about that after my run in with Becky Tahara.

"Yes, you told me that when you called the house."

"May I ask what you do for a living?"

He smiled. "I handle my mother's business and financial affairs. Mine as well. I have a degree in business."

"That pay well?"

Ryan laughed. "There's a ton of investments to manage, and I get one percent of assets as an annual management fee, so I do quite well."

"Do you have a trust fund?"

"No, I don't have a trust fund. Why so much interest in my finances?"

"Since my client is innocent, I'm trying to figure out who might have wanted to harm your father."

He flashed an amused smile. "You think it might have been me?"

"I don't suspect anyone. At this stage, I'm just gathering information."

"I understand. I was also in Hawaii at the time of my father's death, surfing with friends on the north side of Oahu, where the big waves are."

He readily gave me the names and contact info for the friends.

"Who do you think might have wanted your father dead?"

"The list of people who had it in for my father would be very long."

"How so?"

"My father was a mean, tough son-of-a-bitch. He could put on a good face in public. Mr. Perfect, the man of refined taste and manners. But he screwed over and pissed off a lot of folks, and not just in business."

So much for the loving son's starry-eyed image of his dad. My face must have shown my surprise, because Ryan continued, "Look, I have no bad feelings about my father, I got over that a long time ago. I realized early in life that he was a rich prick. I vowed to take full advantage of the rich part and avoid the prick part. I mean, look around you. I have a damn good life. What can I complain about?"

I looked around appreciatively. Super rich seemed pretty good to me, too.

"Anyone in particular your dad pissed off come to mind?

Any threats?"

Christopher returned with our drinks. "Better get us a pitcher of these," Ryan said. "I think Mr. Brink and I are in for a long, private chat." As he went off, Ryan said, "Let me tell you a bit about the Rex Baker enemies list..."

Chapter 9

It was a good hour and several Piña Coladas later—hard to count when they're poured from a pitcher—and Ryan and I were pretty much done, when a stunning, expensively maintained and tastefully bejeweled woman in a yellow silk blouse and tailored tan pants appeared. She looked like an older, female version of Ryan, with the same blond-streaked brown hair, a bit taller than my six feet in her tan sandals.

Ryan rose and hugged her. "Mother, when did you get home?"

"I came in a couple of hours ago."

Ryan introduced me to Danica Baker, Rex Baker's widow. "This is Mr. Brink. He's a detective helping defend the guy accused of killing Rex. He thinks his client is innocent."

Danica Baker had caused a stir when she did not rush home after her husband's death. She was rumored to be out of the country, but where and with whom was subject to much creative writing online. No one seemed able to locate her. Yet here she was. I had once again successfully deployed the private eye's most important tool, dumb luck.

She sat down and eyed the empty pitcher. Ryan got the signal, got up, and said he'd fetch another.

"Yes, Mr. Brink, I just got back in the country. I was on a yacht in the middle of the Pacific Ocean with some friends when we heard the news, and frankly chose not to hurry home. And, no, I was not broken up by the loss of my husband."

I thought it odd that mother and son were so willing to talk to me openly about their dislike for the dearly departed. They also had not argued with my assertion of David's innocence. This was clearly an unusual family.

Ryan returned, trailed by a young woman carrying a tray with a large bowl of peeled shrimp set on top of a stand containing crushed ice, a bowl of cocktail sauce, a plate of lemon wedges, a sliced baguette and a dish of butter. She placed the tray on the table and arranged some linen napkins and silverware that appeared from the pockets of her apron, along with small plates, setting places for two. Ryan filled a clean glass for his mother, refilled mine, and put the pitcher of Piña Coladas down next to the tray. The server, whose name I cleverly deduced was Edita, since that was what mother and son called her, then moved a discrete distance away.

As people who are close often do, Danica and Ryan exchanged a few sentences that I could not follow, but the gist was that Ryan had an early dinner date and would see her later. He politely thanked me for coming and was off.

"This looks like dinner to me," Danica Baker said, eying the shrimp. "My body is still confused about time zones. Would you care to join me?"

I drained my glass, taking care not to slurp with my straw, and was about to pour another when I belatedly remembered the importance of a detective keeping a clear head. "I'd love to, but I'm afraid if I drink any more of these I'll fall asleep."

She laughed. It was a throaty, happy laugh, like she really meant it. "Well, we wouldn't want that! But these won't do that to you. I'm afraid I'm only allowed to drink Virgin Piña Coladas these days."

Mrs. Baker insisted I call her Danica. "Now," she said, with a playful expression, "what shall I call you? Certainly not Mr. Brink."

I was about to say, "Just Brink," but it sounded goofy in my head. I felt my quest to be a last-name-only detective slipping away. Sorry, Spenser. "My name's Joe."

Danica nodded, as if I'd just given the right answer to a tough question. "Yes, Joe Brink. Solid. Masculine. I like it. So, how can I help you, Joe Brink?"

Ok, definitely Joe Brink from now on. Solid and masculine. A good tagline. I made a mental note to get new business cards.

"I'm trying to figure out who else might have wanted to harm your husband. Do you know if he'd received any threats?" Harm, not kill or murder. I was being the tactful, sensitive detective.

Danica spooned some cocktail sauce onto her plate and added a mound of shrimp. She squeezed some lemon juice on top of the sauce, jabbed a shrimp, dipped it into the sauce and popped the whole thing into her mouth. She chewed with obvious pleasure, then wiped a bit of cocktail sauce off the corner of her mouth.

"You go ahead and dig in, Joe Brink. This will take a while."

I was suddenly feeling famished, and a massive peeled shrimp cocktail was very appealing. I almost giggled at my almost pun, and dug in.

Like her son, Danica was unaware of specific threats. She also had a "where shall I begin" list of Rex Baker haters, many of whom overlapped with Ryan's. I was filling my notebook at an unprecedented rate on this case. I was also approaching shrimp cocktail overload.

Edita silently cleared the table and carried away the tray. I noticed that she quickly returned and resumed her position under the shade of a leafy tree, just out of earshot.

Between mother and son, I had a list of way too many people with beefs against Rex Baker, an overabundance of those with motive, and from what I was learning about the victim, there were sure to be more. I would have to focus on means and opportunity to limit the field of suspects to a manageable number.

"Who inherits your husband's estate?"

"Good question, Joe Brink. Who stands to benefit from his death? Except for certain community property, like this place, our son gets everything. Incidentally, my will is the same. It all goes to Ryan"

Ryan Baker had just become very wealthy in his own right. Funny, he didn't mention that. He had just said, nope, no trust fund, answering precisely and unhelpfully the question I had asked.

"Your son said he handled your finances." *And he certainly no longer needs the management fees.*

"He does. My husband married well, Joe. I brought a sizable trust fund and prospects for a large inheritance to the marriage. At the time, Rex was a well-off but not terribly wealthy Silicon Valley marketing guru. I was the rich catch. We have a prenup that, among other things, separated our finances.

"By the time my parents died, and I got that massive inheritance, Rex had become a very wealthy VC. He had also moved on to other women. We kept both our money and our personal lives separate."

"Why did you stay married?" Not so tactful and sensitive, but a private investigator must investigate.

"Why not? We had reached an accommodation early on, and there just seemed to be no reason to divorce."

"You didn't mind other women?"

Danica laughed, again with apparent genuine pleasure. "I stopped caring a long, long time ago. Like I said, that part of our lives was completely separate."

She had not named jealous women when she told me about Rex's enemies. "So, you wouldn't know who he might have been involved with recently?"

"Wouldn't know; wouldn't care. But let me tell you about my husband's harem. He never pursued women. He let them seduce him. He surrounded himself with beautiful women, treated them with disdain, and let those enamored with his wealth and power compete for him. Those that didn't get into the game, he usually replaced. The supply appeared to be endless."

I thought of the three women I had met at the TV studio. They all qualified as exceptionally beautiful. I wondered if they were part of Rex Baker's harem. Especially Misty Morning.

Chapter 10

The Baker estate in Atherton was just minutes from the offices of Rex Baker Venture Partners, located on fabled Sand Hill Road, which runs along the north edge of Stanford University. Also known as VC Row, the one-mile stretch from Interstate 280 on the west to Santa Cruz Avenue on the east, boasts the highest concentration of venture capital firms in the world—several dozen—as well as some of the most expensive office space in the country.

I had a late appointment with Rex Baker's partners, Gavin Smart and Nolan DeWitt. I was sitting in reception promptly at 6 p.m. The lovely, young receptionist—what other kind would Baker hire? —left for the day a few minutes after I arrived. At 6:40, Gavin Smart emerged through the doorway to the offices. I knew it was he because I had not spent the waiting time merely cooling my heels. I had carefully investigated the Rex Baker Venture Partner's brochure and the various PR postings and photos on the waiting room walls, and had detected that Gavin Smart was the completely bald partner.

"Sorry for the wait, Mr. Brink. As you might imagine, things are a bit hectic here."

"No problem," I lied, as he led me into a conference room. Nolan DeWitt was already seated. He put down his iPad and extended his hand across the table. He did not get up.

"Nolan DeWitt."

I shook his hand. "Joe Brink." *Solid and masculine.*

Smart went around to DeWitt's side of the table and sat down, He left an empty chair between them. I sat across from the empty chair.

"I understand you're an investigator for the kid who killed Rex," DeWitt said.

"My client is innocent, and my job is to prove it." I listened to myself say that. Did I believe it? And was I up to proving it? I reminded myself to focus.

"Good that you believe that. Now, how can we help you?"

It was already clear that DeWitt was the alpha dog now. Smart had fetched me, and had remained silent since we entered the room.

"I'm curious. What happens with the business with Mr. Baker gone?"

DeWitt nodded, like he was agreeing that he could tell me that. "Gavin and I are equal partners. We're working out the details of buying out Rex's share from his estate. We have a buy-sell agreement funded by life insurance, so it's mainly a paperwork process."

"How does that work?"

"The company owns an insurance policy. If one of us dies, it pays the company, which uses the funds to buy out the deceased partner."

"What happens with your investors?" That was what I had been asking about. It was obviously not what was most on DeWitt's mind.

Again, that little nod. "We've been doing some hand-holding. There's no issue for the current funds. We'll probably delay starting our next fund until we've booked some great results without Rex."

"What exactly are these funds?"

DeWitt looked at me like I'd just gotten off the boat. This time he shook his head. "Okay. The way VC firms work is that we raise money from investors in funds. Like, we might call a fund we raise this year the 2018 Fund. We manage the fund, invest the money. After a few years, the fund dissolves and the investors divide up the proceeds, less our management fees and incentives."

"So, you'll have a setback without Rex? Need to pay off his estate, no new funds for a while?"

"More of a speed bump."

I looked over at Smart. He was watching DeWitt.

"Will you keep his name?"

"We've just been talking about that. We plan to rebrand after a suitable interval. It'll be DeWitt Smart Venture Partners." For the first time since I came in, DeWitt smiled.

Cute. Many won't even realize there's a Mr. Smart. Score a big one for DeWitt.

"How has the firm been doing?"

"Great!"

"Can you elaborate?"

"No. That information is proprietary."

I looked at him quizzically. He shook his head. "It's private," he said.

"Do you know anyone who had threatened Mr. Baker?"

"No."

"Maybe a disgruntled member of a company you invested in?"

"Nope. Look, this is a business for grownups. We lose everything in a third of our investments; a third more or less break even; a third do well. We have a fiduciary responsibility to our investors to make the tough decisions, and sometimes people get hurt."

I was again puzzled. "Fiduciary?"

DeWitt sighed. "We have to act in our investors' best interests. Which means maximize their returns. Which also means cutting loose losers, be they companies or people."

"I hear partnerships are hard and Mr. Baker could be difficult." I liked my clever choice of the word "difficult." "Did you have any problems with him?"

"None."

"Was he distracted from the firm by his TV show?"

"Nope."

And so it went. After several more negative one-word responses, I got the message. Though he could not resist telling me his name would get first billing when they renamed the firm, DeWitt was not going to reveal anything else, and Smart was mute in his presence. I thanked the partners and took my leave. Smart showed me out.

As we passed through reception, I once more noted the large picture of a smiling Rex Baker on the wall, flanked by smaller photos of Nolan DeWitt and Gavin Smart. I wondered what the photo sizes and arrangement would be after the rebranding.

I also was thinking about how to meet with Gavin Smart alone.

Chapter 11

Guns terrify me. I'm convinced that if I owned a gun, something terrible would happen to me or someone else as a result. So, unlike my fictional detective heroes, I don't use one.

No surprise then that I was duly terrified when two Hispanic men unexpectedly walked into my office first thing in the morning, closed the door, and, while one took a seat across from me at my desk, the other leaned against the door and pointed an immense gun at me. Even if I had a gun nearby and knew how to use it, I would have been scared shitless and paralyzed.

I knew Spenser and Elvis would each maintain his cool in this situation and say something smartass. I was frozen. Struck dumb. I could not take my eyes off that gun and the tattooed hand and arm that held it.

"My name is Navarro Varga," the seated man said. He spoke with a slight Mexican accent, softly and without affect. He reached into his sport coat pocket, withdrew his wallet, removed a $100 bill and placed it down in front of me. My eyes shifted immediately back to the gun. "I wish to engage your services."

I was sweating and about to hyperventilate. Varga said something in Spanish and the gun slowly disappeared inside Tattoo Man's jacket pocket. It was a large pocket. Tattoo

Man crossed his arms and glared at me.

"Perhaps you should have something to drink," Varga said. "You seem agitated."

Varga again spoke in Spanish and Tattoo Man went over to my little refrigerator and got two cans of soda. He handed me one, popped the other, took a long pull, and returned to door guard duty.

I managed to open my can and took a sip. Then I took two more.

"That's better," Varga said. "Now, please give me your cell phone."

I took my phone out of my pants pocket and handed it to him. He satisfied himself it was off, then put it in his pocket and took out his wallet.

"I wish you to find someone for me." He removed a photo from his wallet placed it on top of the hundred. "Her name is Isidora Ramirez. I believe you are acquainted."

I picked up the photo. Yes, I knew her. She was Sofia and Diego's mom. "I can't do this," I croaked.

Navarro's voice became even softer. If anything, it was more menacing. "Yes, you can. She is not your client. Never was, correct? You see, you have no conflict. I *am* your client, and you *will* find her.'

I was unable to formulate a response.

"Perhaps I should be clearer. It is a hazardous world we live in." He placed another photo on top of the first one. My stomach clenched. It was my mom and dad sitting on their tiny front porch. It had a date stamp; it was taken recently. I felt the blood drain from my face.

"Such a devoted son, living with your parents. You must feel a great responsibility to protect them, no? So, we are agreed. I will contact you for a progress report in one week, Señor Héroe Accidental." He tapped my parents' photo twice with his forefinger. "Do not disappoint me."

Navarro Varga rose, took my cellphone out of his pocket and tossed it to me. I caught it reflexively. Tattoo Man opened the door for him, and followed him out. He took his soda can with him.

I went into the bathroom and threw up.

* * *

Sally Rocket taught self-defense. Not martial arts, as she was quick to tell anyone who got the two confused. Sally taught people, mostly teenage girls and women, how to protect themselves. It was all about no-holds-barred street fighting. Her credo was, disable your attacker quickly and get away. She was not into heroics, she was not into winning, she was into escape and survival.

I had met Sally when Curt Kowalski realized I needed to learn to handle myself in a fight. Kowalski-Wu Investigations cases were very white collar, but that did not preclude rough stuff. There was no telling what kind of situation you might find yourself in, and physical violence happened. To me. More than once. After my second hospitalization, Curt sent me to Sally.

I was young and healthy, but neither an athlete nor a fighter. Sally Rocket got me jogging, stretching, and doing some weight lifting. She also taught me how to defend myself.

Which had meant nothing when faced with a gun. Sally did preach that it was always best to avoid a fight, to talk your way out, especially when the odds were against you. I figured two thugs and at least one gun were odds against me.

When I later needed my own office, the space across from Sally' studio had been vacant, so now we were neighbors. I had gone across the hall to her as soon as the goons left and I brushed the puke off my teeth. She was booked all morning. Now we were sharing a pizza for lunch in my office.

"We need to get you a panic button," she said.

"What?"

"Like, under your desk. You press the button, an alarm goes off, I come charging to your rescue."

"You're kidding."

"Okay, now that I'm thinking about it, two buttons. One for a seriously loud alarm, you know, clang-clang-clang. That'll be enough to get a lot of bad guys to split fast. The other silently calls me when I'm across the hall. You can take your pick or use both, depending."

"You aren't kidding."

"The more I think about it, the more I like the idea. You're here all alone. You're a soft target."

"Hey!"

"Don't be offended, tender male ego. Alone is alone. Easy for someone to get the drop on you. Especially easy for more than one someone."

"So, you'll run in with guns blazing?

"I don't even have a gun. I'm just thinking that, in general, I can do rescue."

"I'll think about it, okay?"

"Okay. Now, what about Navarro Varga?"

"Well, after my heart rate settled down, I did some research."

I told Sally what I had learned. I hadn't followed the kidnapping case after the Accidental Hero thing. It had quickly faded from the news. They told me I might be needed as a witness, but nothing ever came of that. Now that I looked, I found a lot of information online.

Jesus Varga had been in the country illegally. Santa Clara may have been a sanctuary county, but when Jesus got his picture plastered all over, ICE came calling. It seemed the county was not about to fight deportation of a notorious kidnapper, and the guy was wanted in Mexico on various serious charges, so he was quickly and quietly turned over to the Mexican Federales.

Meanwhile, according to a small article buried in the local section of the *San Jose Mercury News* a week after the kidnapping rescue story broke, Isidora Ramirez, also undocumented, had disappeared with her two children. It seems that Isidora was convinced that, in the Trump era, all the publicity would bring ICE to her door, she would be sent back to Mexico, and who knew what would happen to her kids? They were both born in San Jose, they were American citizens by right of birth, and she told friends she was sure they would be taken away from her and the kids would disappear into "the system."

I had called Kyle Rizzo, who had been sort of my mentor at Kowalski-Wu, and left a message asking him if he could get a fix on Navarro Varga. I did not tell him why, just that it had something to do with the kidnapping. Just before Sally and I ordered our pizza from MySlice, I received a reply. Navarro Varga was Jesus's smarter, elder brother. He was known to DEA, but had thus far eluded them and all other American law enforcement. He had no record in the

States, not even the proverbial traffic ticket. Navarro routinely travelled to San Jose in the interest of his garden pottery export business.

By the time Sally knew all I knew, our pizza was gone.

"Garden pottery?" she said.

"Garden pottery, my ass."

Chapter 12

Right after lunch, I drove to the Public Defender's office to meet with Sylvia Sanchez.

"How did it go with David?"

"He is one smart dude," she said. "I deal with a lot of street smart guys, but not many like him."

I had not figured David for street smart. "How so?"

"Well, first time we met, I gave him my usual spiel about attorney-client privilege and how it was in his best interest to be completely forthcoming. I also told him I wasn't going to ask him if he 'did it.'"

"Why not?"

"Because sometimes it's in the client's best interest to testify on his own behalf. If I know he's guilty, I can't put him on the stand and have him say he isn't. It's called suborning perjury. So, it's best not to know."

"I see." It was the stock answer, defense lawyer 101, but I had played dumb because I wanted to get Sylvia's take on it. Curt Kowalski had told me that this was his litmus test for whether a defense attorney was ethical. Not the "did you do it" part, the "won't suborn perjury" part. She had passed.

"Anyway, I told him what Hudson Ambrose said. How it was different from what David had told us. Right away, he said that he answered all our questions honestly, but agreed he could have elaborated more, and promised to do better from now on."

"What about his feelings about Rex Baker?"

"He said he didn't know Baker. He wasn't on the board of the failed startup, he was just a worker bee. He didn't know what was going on with investors until the axe fell, and even then, the story was muddled. Of course, he knew the CEO who killed himself, the company only had 20 or so employees, but they weren't close. Said the guy was wound a bit too tight and he could see him cracking from the stress."

"Good answer."

"He also said he and Hudson had decided to take a flyer, applying for the show before they were really ready, but Hudson was sure they'd be in good enough shape to pitch if they got on. David was more cautious, but figured they had nothing to lose by applying."

"What about what Hudson said about him going on the show to turn Baker down?"

"David said he and Hudson agreed Baker would be the wrong investor. He was too old school. They wanted someone younger, more into social media and online sales and marketing." For the first time, she glanced down at her legal pad. "They were hoping for Doreen Sheehan, Bobby Singh or Dusty Brown."

"That makes sense."

"He said he and Hudson did talk about how Baker had screwed over his old company, but he thinks Hudson put two and two together and got five."

"What do you think?" I said.

"I think our boy had awfully good answers."

"I think so too. You think maybe too good?"

"I don't know. I'm lied to so much, it's hard to tell the truth even when I trip over it."

I brought Sylvia up-to-date on my interview with the two *VC Pie* producers, Baker's wife and son, and his former partners. I told her my plan was to focus on exactly how Baker was murdered in order to limit the list of possible suspects. She agreed.

"Did you find out about the camera recordings?" The prosecution's discovery had not included any recordings from the show.

"Yeah," she said, "they said there was some delay reproducing the video file, which is sort of odd, I mean, it's just copying a file, right? Anyway, they said they'd email it before the end of the day."

"That's the video of the actual broadcast?"

Sylvia nodded. "The same one they would normally make available online after the show aired. Only this time, they didn't."

For obvious reasons, although there were homemade videos all over the Internet. "What about the other cameras?" The show used several cameras. In addition to the broadcast, the individual cameras were recorded. They would provide a variety of views, sort of like instant replay. Who knew what we might spot?

"The prosecution doesn't have them. My guess is that the show itself provided the evidence they needed, and they decided not to ask for the others because it couldn't strengthen their case."

"But could weaken it," I said.

"It's possible. The prosecution is required to provide the defense with exculpatory evidence in its possession, but not to go looking for it."

"I'd sure like to see those recordings."

"So would I," Sylvia said. "I'll subpoena them, along with the list of staff who had access to the stage during the time in question. Someone had to swap the green ShushNik for the bomb. Find out who."

Unsaid was that David Novak's life might depend on it. No pressure.

Unless it had been David himself.

Chapter 13

To win the heart of one of my now ex-girlfriends, I once spent a weekend binge-watching episodes of the old TV series *Happy Days* with her. Spend a weekend doing that and you'll really know if you are in love or in lust. I found out it was the latter, and I did not win her heart, but got to sample nearly everything else. We both came away realizing we had little else in common. Not that what we had together was bad, but, hey, I'm maturing.

I was thinking about that as I waited in my office for Kyle Rizzo. Kyle was thin, blue-eyed, with reddish-blond hair, and seemed to be perpetually sunburned, a doppelganger for Richie Cunningham.

Kyle's looks were disarming and deceiving. He had served in special ops in Iran, and been my sort of my big-brother at Kowalski-Wu Investigations, where he was a senior investigator and handled a lot of the riskier, shadier assignments. Kyle once told me he had an Italian-American father and a mother who was a mixture of Puerto Rican, Irish and German. That was how he had become fluent in Italian and Spanish. I had the impression that his father's side of the family in New York was connected, as in Mafia.

When I called Kyle for information on Navarro Varga, he insisted on getting together to find out what was going on.

He said he'd bring lunch from Greasy Jack's if I provided the sodas. I really liked Kyle.

We talked about the Warriors' chances to sweep the playoffs while we dug into our burgers and fries. We agreed that, in addition to being great fun to watch, the Warriors were odds-on favorites for another NBA championship, but a sweep would be tough. Kyle was a long-suffering New York Knicks fan, and I sensed that his heart was not in the conversation.

"Why the interest in Navarro Varga?"

I told Kyle about our meeting. I left out no detail. I showed him the photo of my parents that Varga had left behind. When I finished, he said, "Joe, you are in way over your head."

"Tell me something I don't know."

"I'm afraid there's a lot you don't know." His voice was tinged with regret. "You are involved with some very bad people. You need to take his threat seriously."

"I was afraid of that. Trust me, I am taking it very seriously."

"Remember I told you about my dad's family being involved with the Italian mob?"

I nodded.

"They were gangsters, sure, but they had a code. You went after other wiseguys, fine, that was business. But family was off limits." Kyle shook his head. "But these new guys, they have no boundaries. The Mexican cartels are especially crazy, they have no discipline, no honor."

Varga had ratcheted my anxiety off the charts; Kyle had driven it even higher. "What should I do?"

"Let me make some calls."

* * *

CLANG-CLANG-CLANG. YOUR PHOTO HAS BEEN TRANSMITTED TO THE POLICE. THE POLICE ARE ON THEIR WAY. CLANG-CLANG-CLANG.

"That'll scare the crap out of Vu and Chu," I said.

"If they're ever here when we use it," Sally said.

We had just tested our new security and panic systems. It had taken us all afternoon to install them. It was Sally's afternoon off. She and I had set up similar systems in my office and her studio.

We had also warned the fro-yo shop and bakery before running the test. The folks who worked there thought it was cool.

We both now had a custom, do-it-yourself system, with the usual security cameras for the hall and inside the office, door and window sensors, and a motion detector. But the big deal was the panic system, which included a big bell on the wall that made a deafening clang. There was a strobe light that flashed to reinforce the "your photo has been transmitted to the police" announcement. There was a panic button under my desk, and Sally had a couple of them strategically placed in her studio. When I pushed my button, the alarm went off, the light flashed, and Sally's bell clanged as well to summon her. And vice-versa. We each also had a silent button to call each other for help. There was also a phone app with integrated text messaging and a host of other features.

The only thing was, the police were not actually called. Nor did either of us opt for the 24/7 monitoring service; the monthly charges were too high.

At the same time, I had finally broken down and gotten my own Internet service. Sally and I had both been piggybacking off the frozen yogurt shop's public Wi-Fi. It was slow, but, worse, had no security. I'd had the cable company in and now had a fast cable router that also ran my office phone. While Sally and I were running wires for the security system in the space above the dropped ceiling, I ran an ethernet cable from my new router over to Sally's studio and added her own router. We had agreed to share the monthly cost of the Internet service.

In a couple of days, my folks were having a more traditional home security system installed by a major national company. It was a gift from me, though they were paying for the monitoring service. I didn't tell my parents why I wanted them to get a security system, but they thought it was sweet that I, their son the expert, the professional PI, cared so much about them, and their loving son had left it at that.

I wasn't sure if any of this would help with Navarro Varga, but I felt a little better. At least I had done something.

* * *

The lead story on the front page of the local section of the newspaper next morning was about a big fire overnight at the police lab. They were already calling it arson. It must have been a doozy, because it had gone to multiple alarms and the article was accompanied by a photo showing huge flames.

The article said the fire was set in the storage area and much of the evidence stored there had been destroyed. It also quoted unnamed sources as saying it looked gang-related, like an attempt at screwing up one or more gang member cases. I wondered how you could tell a fire was gang-related. I called Sylvia and asked what this meant to our case.

"Well, the bomb evidence was in storage there, and from what I hear, it's gone."

"So that's good for us, right?"

"Not so much. I'll probably be able to get the lab report thrown out, but so what? The prosecution doesn't need an analysis of the bomb to make their case that there was one. Millions saw it. It's sort of like not having the weapon, but capturing the shooting and shooter on video; you can still get a conviction without it."

Chapter 14

"I think Hung Chu is planning to kill me."

Minh Vu was seated across from me in my office. He was a small, thin, sad looking man I figured for mid-60s, and sat still and erect. It was the first time I had seen my office neighbor in weeks. Our previous conversations had been limited to variations of "hello" spoken in passing.

"That sounds like a police matter."

Mr. Vu extended his hands, palm out, fingers up, and shook them side-to-side. "No, no, no police."

"What do you think I can do for you?"

"I want to know if it is true, but I do not want him to know I suspect him. In case I am mistaken."

I was working the Perfect Murder case pro bono, as in free, as in no income. It looked like it would be a long slog, and I needed to make some money. I had picked up a couple of cheating spouse cases, but was reluctant to turn away more paying business. "I would be happy to help you if I can. Please tell me more."

We PIs are expert interviewers, but this was not an investigatory interview. This was the sort of situation where you want to hear from your client in their own words, in their own way. So, for now, I would let Mr. Vu talk, using questions only to help keep him going.

"Chu and I are financial advisors."

I nodded sagely at this revelation, though I had already detected that. It said so on their door: Minh Vu, Hung Chu, Financial Advisors.

"Our clients are mostly older Vietnamese who came here as boat people, as we did. They are more comfortable talking about money to someone who understands their culture and speaks their language. More trusting as well."

I smiled and nodded. I knew that, to southeast Asians, this signified that I was respectfully listening, not necessarily that I was agreeing.

"We work mostly in the evenings and on weekends. It is when our clients are available."

Which explained why they were rarely here when I was, which was mostly weekdays.

"Chu and I have worked together for more than 20 years. Recently, I noticed he was behaving strangely."

"How so?"

"Sometimes, clients come for appointments but he is not here. This never happened before. Some complained to me that he was neglecting their accounts, but what could I do?"

"Are you partners?"

"We do not have a formal partnership. We share the rent and office expenses. But we are otherwise independent. He has his office and clients, I have mine."

"Why do you think he plans to kill you?"

"He wants me out of the way so he can expand his drug business."

Whoa, I did not see that coming. I meant to ask Mr. Vu what made him think Mr. Chu was planning to kill him, not why. Sometimes you get better answers when you ask imprecise questions.

"He sells drugs?"

"I think he must. I think he is now using the investment business as a front. He wants me gone so he can have the whole suite and expand his drug business. It would be easier for him, he would not have to hide it from me."

"Has he been involved with drugs before?"

"Not that I know about. But he is a private person, and I have always respected his privacy."

"Is there something specific that makes you think he plans to kill you."

"I do not think he plans to do it himself. I think he plans to have me killed."

Patience. "What exactly makes you think that?"

"I went into his office last night. We keep our offices locked, but have keys in case of an emergency. I have never done this before, but I was overcome by suspicion. Chu is a meticulous man, or was, but his desk was a mess. Right on top, I found the evidence."

"What evidence?"

"A photo of me with my name written on the back, along with my home address and phone numbers, and my usual office hours."

"And you think that means what?"

"I think he will give that to one of his drug hoodlums to use to identify me and kill me."

"Any other evidence?"

"Unusual credit card charges. You see, we use a business credit card. They give us separate account numbers but one invoice to pay. We do it for the cash-back rewards. The bill comes to me, I give Chu his list of charges for his records, and we send them two checks. But when I started getting suspicious a couple of months ago, I looked at his charges. See for yourself."

Mr. Vu handed me a few sheets of paper he had been holding in his left hand. They were copies of Mr. Chu's credit card bill for each of the last two months. He pointed out several Uber charges, two each Thursday.

"Doesn't he drive?"

"He stopped driving a few months ago. He said it was to save money, but I believe it was to fool anyone trying to follow him to his drug sales."

"I'd like to make a copy of these."

"Please keep them. I feel ashamed to be spying on my friend."

The friend who you think wants to have you killed. "I'll look into this."

"Please, I do not want Mr. Chu to think I do not trust him."

But you don't trust him. "I'll be discreet."

"There is another thing. He now avoids talking to me. He will not look me in the eye. I think he is dishonored by his evil ways and cannot face me."

"What do you think caused this change?"

"Who is to know such things? For years, he was a good, reliable associate. We had no conflicts. Perhaps it is loneliness."

"He's alone?"

"His wife died a couple of years ago. Brain aneurysm. They had no children and he has no close family."

Mr. Vu had run out of things to tell me and I had run out

of questions. I signed up my new client and got a check for a retainer.

I wanted to search Mr. Chu's office, and Mr. Vu said Mr. Chu almost never showed up during the day. So, with Mr. Vu as my lookout, I did just that.

Was that kosher? I don't know. I figured Vu's name was on the lease and he had the key to Mr. Chu's office, so I assumed he had permission to enter it, and then he invited me in...

In other words, I rationalized.

Mr. Chu's office was, as Mr. Vu had described it, a mess. It looked like no files had been put away for some time, they were strewn all over, and his desk looked like a paper recycling dumpster.

I dug around and found a sheet of paper helpfully labelled "passwords." I downloaded a bunch of files from his hard drive to a thumb drive. I knew a lot of this was confidential client information, and I planned to delete anything not relevant to the investigation as soon as I had determined what was.

I saw the photo that had upset Mr. Vu. It was eight-by-ten, centered on top of the desktop pile.

The other papers were unrevealing, and the desk and file drawers were locked. I did not possess lock-picking skills, so I left them alone, and left Mr. Chu's office.

Later, after a couple of hours spent looking at spreadsheets—it seemed Mr. Chu did everything in Excel—I had found nothing that would indicate a drug business. All there was were client records and Mr. Chu's business records. The latter were bland, though I thought it was odd that there were few entries for this year.

I kept some of the files just in case I needed to go back over them and jettisoned the rest. I felt I had not unduly infringed on Mr. Chu's clients' privacy.

The big payoff was that I had made a copy of Mr. Chu's passwords. I wanted to know where he had gone on all those Uber trips. I could not use his Uber password to get to his ride history. Uber, like many online services, used two-factor authentication. That meant that when you logged in, you had to enter a code that was sent to you via email or text. This prevented someone who knew your password from logging in. It foiled a lot of hacking based on stolen passwords.

But I had Mr. Chu's email password, and he had not enabled two-factor authentication on his email account. I was able to log into his account on my computer and look at his emails from Uber, which they send after every trip. Better yet, Mr. Chu seemed to never delete emails, his inbox had thousands of them. A quick search and I had all the Uber emails. Soon, I had a list of all the trips.

In each case, he had started at home on a Thursday afternoon and gone someplace in the Bay Area. A few hours later, he'd return. I began looking up the addresses on Google Maps. It was painstaking, but the pattern was soon clear.

I also found out from emails why Mr. Chu had stopped driving. He'd had a series of accidents, lost his auto insurance, and his driver's license had been suspended. Was Mr. Chu using? Drinking? There was nothing to indicate either of these.

Mr. Chu's emails did not shed any light on the reason for his Thursday outings, nor did they indicate any hint of a drug business, or anything else nefarious.

I had some useful information, maybe even clues, but

what did they mean? That flurry of minor auto accidents gave me a hunch. I had seen that happen before. I did not want to jump to conclusions, but, if I was right, I needed to move fast.

Chapter 15

I once asked Curt Kowalski what I should do if I got stuck on a case. He said, "You're an investigator. You investigate!"

That's what Spenser and Elvis did. They poked around and annoyed people until somehow a clue emerged. I could do that, too.

Mr. Vu had decided, with my encouragement, to take a vacation out of town while I worked out a plan for Mr. Chu. I had gotten the goods on my errant spouses—as usual, logs of assignations and compromising photos. Meanwhile, David Novak was still in jail facing a murder trial, and I felt I had to do something for him while I was waiting for the camera recordings in response to our subpoena.

Gavin Smart said he would meet me at a sandwich shop near my office that had tables next to the sidewalk out front. He was late, but I didn't mind. I was girl watching, like Spenser did on Boylston and Berkeley in Boston. He was always admiring the young women in their summer dresses. We were having a warm spring day, but California girls do not take to summer dresses. Still, skinny jeans or shorts and tank tops provide ample opportunities for them to display their charms, and I was an appreciative spectator.

I wanted to talk to Smart because he had been mum in the presence of his domineering partner, Nolan DeWitt. I had no idea what he might have to say that would be helpful, if anything, but at least I was investigating.

"Thanks for meeting me here," I said, as he walked up and sat down across from me. I figured he wanted to meet in downtown Campbell because it was unlikely anyone who knew him and DeWitt would see him there. Wedged between sprawling San Jose and tony Los Gatos, the small city of Campbell was like a distant country to the denizens of Sand Hill Road.

"Glad to save you a trip."

We went inside and ordered our lunches. We chose different grilled cheese something-or-others. They gave us a plastic thing with a number on it to put on our table so someone could bring us our food, and mugs so we could get fountain drinks for ourselves.

Once seated again, I wanted to know why Smart had agreed to see me. "Why did you agree to see me?"

"My partner likes to control conversations," he said.

"I noticed."

"He's a decent guy, but even more of a control freak than Rex was, if that's possible."

"So, what did you not get to say?"

"Look, I'm not saying Rex was an easy man to like or even work with, he wasn't, but he was good to me. I was a junior analyst at an investment bank when Rex hired me back when he was getting started. He gave me the opportunity to get to where I am now. He was difficult and demanding, but he made me step up my game every day. I've done very well and wouldn't be where I am if not for Rex Baker."

A young guy with a man bun and tattoo sleeves served us our sandwiches and chips. I wondered if he had thought about wearing those tats for the rest of his life when he got them. I realized that his concept of the future was probably measured in weeks. It made me feel old.

We ate a while. Smart's tribute to Rex Baker had to be leading somewhere, and I debated how to get him to spit it out. Sometimes, letting the interviewee fill the silence is a good tactic, especially when you don't know what to say. So, I focused on chewing.

"You probably wonder where this is going."

I am such a clever interviewer. "I do."

"Have you met Mrs. Baker?"

"Yes, I have."

"What did you think of her?"

"Gracious. Charming. Why?"

"What about her son?"

"I'd say the same about him."

"That they are," he said. "They're also in deep financial trouble, or were before Rex died. Now all that's changed."

Yowsa! A clue!

"How do you know that?"

"My office is right next to Rex's. When he's excited, he yells, and I can hear him. The last few months, he was yelling a lot."

"Who was he yelling at?"

"Ryan. Sometimes on the phone. Twice, the kid came to see him."

"What were they talking about?"

"I couldn't hear Ryan. His voice was too soft, and he seemed to stay calm. And most of it was phone calls. But Rex would just go ballistic. Like, 'How could you do that?' and 'Didn't you ever hear of due diligence?' and 'Why didn't you come to me sooner?' There was also a lot of general cursing. I especially remember hearing 'Ryan, you fucking moron' a lot."

I nodded. I made a mental note to look up "due diligence."

"Anything else you remember?"

"That's about it."

"Do you recall specific dates?"

"Not really. But I think it started right after New Year's. I remember thinking about how people wait until after the holidays to deal with family shit. It sort of stopped a month or so ago. Just before, you know..."

"Did Rex ever talk about it?"

"Not that I heard. It wouldn't have been like him to do that, he didn't talk about personal stuff."

We finished lunch. Gavin Smart appeared to be distracted. He did not seem to appreciate the girl watching opportunity.

Chapter 16

I looked up due diligence. The definitions all used fancy language that netted down to this: be sure you know what you're getting into. For investments, it means digging into and verifying financial and other relevant information before you invest. Buyer beware.

I regularly watched this TV show where a guy goes around investing in struggling small businesses and works to revive them. Then, after he's done the deal, he finds out important stuff he didn't know when he invested, like the partners hate each other, or they had lost their biggest customer, or they lost their lease, that sort of thing. I always found myself yelling at the screen, "Why didn't you do better investigation?" Now I could yell, "Why didn't you do better due diligence?"

No surprise, there was no information online about Danica's and Ryan's financial affairs, so I called Sylvia Sanchez and persuaded her to authorize DeepDig reports. If what Gavin Smart told me was true, mother and son had a few hundred million good reasons to want Rex Baker dead, on top of their general and freely expressed dislike of the man they respectively, if not respectfully, called husband and father.

* * *

The local office of Yuanxing Foundry was in Sunnyvale, a 15 minute straight shot up 85. A quick online search revealed that the Chinese firm specialized in developing prototypes for tech devices. Yuanxing had built all the ShushNiks. The Silicon Valley office housed local sales and sales engineering staff.

I went through the security-reception ritual, got a visitor's badge, and was soon greeted by a young Chinese looking man who introduced himself as Sammy Fan.

"Thanks for seeing me on such short notice, Mr. Fan" I said.

"No problem, I happened to be free this afternoon. And call me Sammy."

As we went through the small lobby, Sammy said, "You probably didn't read the fine print on the sign-in sheet. No one does. Everything we do here is proprietary to someone, and when you signed in, you agreed to honor that. That means no photos, no copying documents, that sort of thing. I'm responsible for you, so please respect that."

"Sure. I'm only interested in matters that pertain to our investigation."

When I called, I identified myself as an investigator on the David Novak case. I did not mention that I worked for the defense.

We reached a cubicle in a warren of a couple of dozen. Sammy sat behind his desk, I sat across from him. "Would you mind showing me some ID?"

I flashed my PI license, complete with my photo. It was a practiced move in which I flipped open my wallet and held it with my finger over the word "private." That seemed to satisfy him.

Time to loosen him up by getting him to talk about something easy. "Would you tell me what you folks do?"

"Sure. Our tagline is, 'We take your idea from concept to reality.' Wherever you are in your device development process, whether it's just a sketch on a napkin or a functioning model, we work with you to refine the design by building prototypes. We can also handle small-scale manufacturing, and when you're ready, we facilitate the handoff to a large-scale manufacturer."

It was a well-rehearsed elevator pitch, nicely delivered. "So that's what you did for ShushTek."

"Yes. It was a very successful project. They were about ready to go into mass production when..."

His voice tailed off as he struggled to find the right sales guy words. I jumped to the rescue. "Yes, it was a tragedy. I understand that you folks built the five colored devices for the show."

"That's right, and I can assure you, they were all exactly to spec. And we only made ShushNiks for ShushTek as they ordered them. That's tightly controlled."

"Don't worry, no one thinks your company had anything to do with what happened. But I'm curious. If I wanted to, how would I make a ShushNik case?"

"If you knew the specs or had one of them, you could do it with a 3-D printer. That's how we make them."

"You mean anyone could do it?"

"Well, you'd need the right kind of 3-D printer, and, like I said, either a model or the specs. But, yeah, it wouldn't be that hard."

"Would that include the screen and power button?"

"No, but they're off-the-shelf parts."

"Off-the-shelf?"

Sammy laughed. "Off the right shelf. What I mean is that they're standard parts, commercially available from any number of suppliers. You wouldn't have to build them."

"Could I buy them?"

"Sure. Look, this stuff isn't a secret."

He looked something up on his computer, with the screen angled so I couldn't see it. Then he wrote something on his yellow pad, tore the sheet off and handed it to me.

"These are the part and model numbers. If you had the case, these would complete the exterior."

"Thanks. While you're at it, I need copies of all the ShushTek orders."

"Sorry, that's confidential."

"Okay, I get that." It had been worth a shot.

We chatted for a while longer, but I already had what I came for, though not what I had hoped for. The field of suspects was still wide open.

From the parking lot, I emailed Sylvia and asked her to get a subpoena for the ShushTek orders. I didn't really expect to find anything as obvious as an order for another green ShushNik, but you can never tell. I had to close that loop.

Chapter 17

When I first started at Kowalski-Wu, I met Ricky Clancy. Ricky was a few years older than me, and did occasional gofer work for the agency, pickup and delivery kinds of things. He worked as an independent contractor, while I was an official apprentice and employee. Still, gofering was the start of my training, and Ricky taught me the ropes. He also drove for Uber, his fulltime job that enabled him to be on call for the agency on an as-needed basis.

This Thursday afternoon, Ricky was working for me. He was parked in the lot of the Home Depot that was less than five minutes from Mr. Chu's condo complex. You could sit in your car in a Home Depot lot for hours and no one would notice, let alone think anything of it. If the pattern held, sometime between 2 and 4 p.m. Mr. Chu would hail Uber. The plan was for Ricky to grab the trip and text me the destination.

At 3:10, my phone chimed. Ricky was driving Mr. Chu to Stoneridge Mall in Pleasanton. I went across the hall and got Sally—it was again her afternoon off—and we were soon heading out 280 to 680 for the 45-minute drive.

Whatever Mr. Chu was doing each Thursday for the past two months, he had been doing it at a different Bay Area shopping mall each time. From his Uber email receipts, I had made a list of them, along with the dates and times. Stoneridge would be a new addition to the list.

We got to the Stoneridge parking lot, I parked my Prius, and Sally and I got in position inside the mall. I texted Ricky, who replied with a thumbs-up emoji. He had gone the speed limit and was just arriving. I'd gone with the left lane traffic, which flowed 10-15 miles an hour faster.

We were concerned that Mr. Chu might recognize us, so Sally and I wore bland hoodies without insignias, with the hoods over our heads. Dark sunglasses completed the disguises. It would be hard for our best friends to tell who we were.

We were waiting near the entrance at which Ricky planned to drop off Mr. Chu. He texted that Mr. Chu was entering. I was window shopping with a view of the entrance, and picked him up as he came inside. As Ricky had texted, Mr. Chu was wearing gray chinos and a white dress shirt under a black windbreaker. He carried nothing.

I texted Ricky that we had the target in sight, and thanked him. His role in the exercise was over.

From her position across the aisle, Sally gave me the thumbs-up, signifying that she had spotted Mr. Chu as well. It would be the last time we would acknowledge each other. We would stay in contact on our phones. With about half the shoppers in the mall on their phones, this would be inconspicuous.

For the next four hours, we tag-teamed Mr. Chu. He was doing what you would expect if he was trying to detect or lose a tail. He'd walk into a shop, then immediately walk out, only to return to the same store later and comb the aisles. He went up an escalator, then immediately down again. He used the elevator, and different restrooms on different floors. He entered every type of shop, large and small, and spent a good fifteen minutes checking out every table and line in the food court. Wherever he went, he didn't seem to look at the merchandise, but was constantly scanning the shoppers.

The hardest thing about tailing someone is not being able to pee, and we almost lost him when I had to take a quick potty break just before Mr. Chu decided to double back and plunge into the bustling Nordstrom crowd. Sally barely managed to keep track of him from a discreet distance until I responded to her text telling me his location and was back on track.

Mr. Chu did not interact with anyone that either of us noticed, and we'd had him under constant surveillance except for his two trips to the restroom. I did not want to risk following him there.

The outer reaches of a dark mall parking lot were a perfect place for a quick, clandestine, illicit transaction. It appeared that would be the endgame of all this tradecraft. Sure enough, a few minutes after eight o'clock, as darkness fell, Mr. Chu headed for an exit.

Darkness works both ways. It would be hard to tail him but also hard for him to pick us up. But that turned out to be moot. Mr. Chu stopped just inside the exit and fiddled with his phone. A few minutes later, he went out to the curb and got into a car with an Uber logo in the window.

Later, my email snooping would verify that he went straight home. Sally and I were stumped. Had he done some sort of slick transaction that had eluded us? He had not been out of sight of at least one of us for more than a few seconds at a time. Even his trips to the restroom were brief. He never had anything in his hands. And there was no sign that he had detected us.

What was with these odd mall excursions?

Chapter 18

The financial section of the DeepDig report on Danica Baker made for fascinating reading.

Danica's father, Laszlo Szarka, came to America in 1957 as a refugee from the aborted 1956 Hungarian Revolution, after the Soviet Union sent in tanks and crushed the student-led rebellion against the communist regime. The young man's role in the uprising was not revealed, but he ended up in the Midwest, working in a small department store in farm country.

By 1970, Szarka owned the store. When he was bought out by a private equity firm in the early 1980s, he had a chain of 12 department stores.

Danica was Szarka's only child, and she inherited his fortune when her parents died in an auto accident in 1989. Not long afterward, she married Rex Baker and the couple had their only child in 1993.

At the time of their marriage, Danica's net worth was estimated to be $20 million. Rex Baker was just building his reputation as a Silicon Valley marketing genius. Though the report did not state it, I doubted he was worth a million dollars at the time.

While Rex's star and wealth rose, Danica Baker stuck with the conservative Midwest financial advisor who had managed her father's money. Her separate wealth, as specified in the couple's prenuptial agreement, had grown to approximately $80 million by 2015. That year, according to the report, Ryan Baker assumed the role of financial manager and began redeploying funds more aggressively. The report concluded by stating that, "Results since Ryan Baker assumed control are unavailable, and we are unable to estimate the current value of the portfolio."

DeepDig was notorious for being able to get private financial information. I wondered if Ryan had intentionally hidden those financial results. Had he gambled with his mother's money and lost? That would support Gavin Smart's contention that Danica and Ryan were going broke before Ryan inherited his father's fortune.

Danica Baker did not seem like a fool to me. Quite the opposite. How, I wondered, had she let her neophyte son wipe out an $80 million investment portfolio? If that was what had happened. It was pure conjecture, based on Smart's report of one side of overheard conversations.

I also recalled that both Danica and Ryan had airtight alibis, not only for the day of the murder, but for the week before as well. Of course, that didn't much matter. It's not like either of them would have gone into the studio and planted the bomb. If one or both of them were behind this, who was their accomplice? Who made the switch? That remained the big question. How was I going to figure that out?

* * *

Rex Baker had written a book, one of those ghostwritten vanity pieces for the rich and famous. It was a collection of unrelated chapters recounting the glories of his rags-to-riches career. Self-serving though it was, I felt I was gaining insight into him as I read it.

Unlike many VCs, Rex Baker chased profit, not revenue. He invested in high-end, high-margin businesses, and had nothing but disdain for mass-market products, which he characterized as "rush to the bottom." He said that the Internet had made low-price-chasing so easy for customers, it had squeezed the profit out of commoditized products.

Early in his career, Baker was a protégé of Steve Jobs. He admired how Apple avoided the commodity PC market and managed to command higher prices, and thus margins, for its Macintosh computers.

While the other VCs on *Venture Capital Pie* would press entrepreneurs about how they could lower their price, usually by getting to higher volume production and moving manufacturing offshore, Rex Baker was the contrarian. He would occasionally make deals for something he viewed as a commodity, but his condition was always that it be a licensing play. Rake in royalties while others used the invention in their product line. But the deals he really liked were the ones where he would say, "I'll do this deal, but under one condition. You abandon your mass-market strategy and let me take you up-market."

He had followed this approach at Rex Baker Venture Partners. I had just read the chapter about how, while others were chasing volume in the home and business security device market, he had gone after companies at the high-end. He had also invested in companies under the same condition he often touted on *VC Pie*, that they abandon the low-end and go up-market.

This got me thinking. All the security gear Sally and I had just installed were commodities. We had ordered the stuff online, and mainly shopped for price and free shipping. Which got me to thinking about some of the cool but expensive gear we had come across, like the cameras that were so tiny you could put them anywhere and no one would notice them. Of course, in our case, we wanted the cameras to be visible. We wanted the bad guys to know they were being recorded.

Which got me right on the phone to Sylvia Sanchez. "We need another subpoena for all the security recordings at the *VC Pie* studio. Inside and outside."

"I thought you said there weren't any security cameras on the set."

"I saw cameras in the hall and outside, but none on the set. But just because I didn't see them doesn't mean they weren't there."

I explained about Rex Baker's investments in companies with high-end security equipment, like pinhead cameras. "And he was a control freak. He just may have had hidden cameras on the set."

"It's worth a shot," Sylvia said.

Chapter 19

I rang Mr. Chu's doorbell just before 6 p.m. I was holding a pizza box. If he was a vicious drug dealer, I might be about to get my head blown off.

The door opened slowly, halfway. Mr. Chu looked timid and surprised. As I'd guessed, there was not a hint of recognition on his face. Nor viciousness.

"Yes?"

I held out the box. "Here's your pizza."

"Did I order a pizza?"

"Your name is Chu? This is unit 2B?"

"Yes, but..."

"Can I bring it inside?"

Mr. Chu looked confused, but he let me push the door open and come in.

It was not what I expected. The place was neat and tidy. But the other clues were obvious. I needed to bring in the authorities.

I put the pizza on the small table in the dining area outside the kitchen. "How about we share this?"

Mr. Chu silently sat at the table. I went into the kitchen and sent a quick text message, then came out with plates and utensils. "What can I get you to drink?"

"A can of soda, please."

I opened the fridge and took out two cans of some generic cola. I had no idea what toppings Mr. Chu might prefer, so I had brought a plain cheese pizza. He ate slowly, but with obvious enjoyment. I joined him, feeling profoundly sad. We ate in silence.

The pizza was cut into six slices. Just as I finished my third slice, the doorbell rang. I rose right away. "Let me get it."

I opened the door. Sally smiled at me, then stepped aside. A man and woman of Vietnamese descent smiled at me. I showed them in. Mr. Chu looked up from his pizza.

"Mr. Chu," I said, "these people are here to help you."

* * *

After Grandma died, my grandfather, my mother's father, lived with us for about a year. I was mostly away at college, but soon realized he had Alzheimer's. Grandma had taken care of him, and he was lost without her.

My parents were of a culture and generation that was into heavy denial about such things. Grandpa started wandering away from the house, looking for Grandma and unable to find his way back home. He put Post-It Notes on his dresser drawers that told him what was inside, even one on the outside of the door to his room with his name on it. Ultimately, Mom and Dad had to put Grandpa into a nearby memory care nursing home. It was not safe to leave him alone.

He's still there. What I remember the most about the first time I visited him was how relaxed Grandpa looked. He still knew who I was then. Now, when I visit, I have to remind him who I am, and I'm not sure it completely registers.

When Sally told me about her encounter with Mr. Chu the other day, I experienced déjà vu. She was leaving her studio for the day, walking to her car, when she saw him walking along Campbell Avenue. He was staring at a building a few doors down from ours. When she approached and greeted him, he looked startled, and asked her how she knew his name.

Sally explained who she was, that she worked right across the hall from his office. He asked her if she would take him there. Sally realized he couldn't find our building.

It confirmed my earlier hunch about the traffic accidents. Like Grandpa, Mr. Chu could no longer drive because of them. Alzheimer's can do that to you.

He also kept forgetting appointments and commitments to clients. He had Mr. Vu's picture on his desk, with his name and address written on it, so he could remember who his friend and partner for so many years was.

Every Thursday, Mr. Chu went to a different mall, spent several hours, then returned home. After the Stoneridge Mall escapade, I had called Mr. Vu with a question. He told me that, yes, Mrs. Chu had collapsed one evening at a shopping mall, alone, while her husband was at work. He had dropped her off there and planned to pick her up after his last appointment. Instead, he got a call from the police, and by the time he got to the hospital, she was gone.

When I went to Mr. Chu's home, he had not recognized me any more than he had when he'd met Sally. When he let me inside, there were Post-It Notes everywhere, with all sorts of reminders. I later learned that he had a weekly maid service and she had been there that day, which explained the tidy order in his home as compared to the chaos in his office.

Sally and I left Mr. Chu with the two social workers from a county-funded program that worked with elderly Vietnamese-Americans with dementia, Alzheimer's and other mental health issues. They usually helped families deal with their aging loved one, but Mr. Chu had no family. I called Mr. Vu and explained the situation. He said he would return from his vacation and help his old friend.

Chapter 20

I started the morning with the security video Sylvia Sanchez had subpoenaed. Unfortunately, there had been no security camera on the set. I spent an hour looking at what we received, but it was all from the outer hallway, and I saw nothing useful.

They used three cameras to shoot *Venture Capital Pie*, and I also had the footage from each of them, delivered in response to our earlier subpoena. I had repeatedly watched the live broadcast video, which contained cuts among all three cameras. Now, I repeated that process for each of the individual cameras.

It was all of three minutes from the time David Novak was introduced until the fatal explosion. I watched at normal speed. Slow motion. Freeze this frame or that. Advance frame by frame. Go back a few. Looking for...that's the thing, I didn't know what I was looking for. Something, anything that was unusual. I was waiting for something to jump out at me and announce itself as a clue.

The cameras from stage right and center stage were unrevealing. The stage-left camera had focused on the VCs, until Rex moved to center stage. It then focused on him in those final seconds as he faced David, hunched his shoulders, dipped his head towards the ShushNik in his hand, and pressed the button. This was the same shot that had been broadcast live. It was awful and yet compelling footage, ending when the shockwave hit the camera and knocked it and the cameraman over. But it offered no clues.

I went back to study the video from the stage-right camera again. A half-hour later, I was convinced that either David was innocent or he was one of the world's best actors. He looked completely unaware that a tragedy was imminent, right up until the end. The problem was, sociopaths often are great actors, and I could not dismiss the possibility that David might be one.

A morning spent staring fruitlessly at the videos had given me a headache, the kind that only a hearty lunch can cure. I went out in search of a chocolate shake, double-cheeseburger, and fries. I was a firm believer in medicinal meals.

* * *

While I was finishing my medicine at Greasy Jack's, I got a text from Misty Morning.

Misty: Did you hear?
Me: Hear what?
Misty: Need to see you
Me: Sure, where?
Misty: I'll come to you

I rushed back to my office to get it ready for company. When I got there, I realized there wasn't much to do. Looking at it as if with fresh eyes, I realized my office was minimalist. As in bare but functional. Or was it barely functional? I tidied up a bit, which took less than a minute.

Then I waited, edgy as a teenager for a first-time date.

When Misty arrived, I held her chair for her while she sat down, then sat next to her instead of behind my desk. She looked great, if you didn't notice that her eyes were red, like she'd been crying. They also didn't look quite so big this time.

"Have you been crying?"

She took a tissue from her handbag and dabbed at her eyes. "I'm sorry."

"What for?"

"I'm being so wimpy."

"About what?"

"It's just so unfair!"

I was not making great headway detecting. Time to take a different tack. "Tell me what happened. Start at the beginning."

Misty softly blew her nose, sat up straight and tried to compose herself. But she was wringing the poor tissue with both hands.

"Well. You know that the network owns the show now? They're moving it down to Burbank? They just announced that Storm will be the new host and made Becky the new executive producer?"

I remembered that Becky Tahara had told me about the network exercising their option to buy the show from Rex Baker's estate and probably moving it. The rest was new information. The statements-as-questions somehow were not so adorable this time. In fact, they were annoying. But, good detective that I am, I nodded sympathetically, waiting for Misty to get to the 'so what.'"

The tears started again. The mangled tissue was exchanged for a fresh one, which was put to immediate use on her eyes.

"The bitch fired me," Misty hissed. Her eyes were like slits.

It was not a sound I imagined coming from her pretty lips, yet it just had. I checked. There was no one else around.

"Did she give you a reason?"

"Just some bullshit about using staff from the Burbank studio, and me being redundant. Redundant? Can you believe that fucking shit?"

And a potty mouth, too. My illusions of an angel were crumbling.

Misty gave me a questioning look. But I didn't know what the question was. Surely, she did not want my opinion about the bitch and her shit. And what had happened made sense to me. This made it hard to answer, so I didn't. I once more went for sympathetic.

"That's awful. I'm so sorry for you." I resisted the temptation to pat her arm or hand, and a comforting hug would have been awkward the way we were seated in adjacent chairs.

It seemed I had given the correct answer, because Misty brightened considerably. "Thank you. Now it's my turn."

For what?

"She thinks she's done with me. She made a big mistake."

I smelled revenge.

"How so?"

"If I don't work there, I don't have to do what they want? Like, I can help you?"

"I'd be glad for any help you can give me."

"You asked about who had access to the set?"

"I did."

"And Becky sent you a long list?"

"Yes."

"I heard her talking to someone on the phone about it, a lawyer? Anyway, the list is bullshit. They decided to give you everyone who could have possibly been on the set that day. Not who actually was."

"Can you help narrow it down?"

Misty bit her lower lip and smiled. Her eyes seemed to have recovered. "You bet I can. You got the security camera video from outside? But none from the set? That's because Becky doesn't know about that." She smiled wickedly. "But I do."

Chapter 21

"You know the real reason the bitch fired me? Because I took Rex away from her?" Misty looked triumphant. This woman changed moods on a dime.

My Misty with Rex Baker? It felt creepy. But before I got lost in tales of the harem, I wanted to know about that camera. "Tell me about the security camera."

"Not camera. Cameras. Rex couldn't talk to her about tech stuff, the bitch can barely work her phone. But with me he was, like, cloud and wireless and all that."

"Where were they?"

"The cameras? In the vents, over the control room windows? It was, like, a secret? For security? Like, what good would it be if everyone knew?"

I remembered the layout. The control room faced the set, with floor-to-ceiling windows giving the crew a full view. The control room was a big box. The set had a much higher ceiling with all sorts of gear up there that you never saw on TV, and there was ductwork with vents that ran along the front of the control room roof.

I listened with half an ear as Misty prattled on about all the ways Rex had found her so much more appealing than Becky. I was now experiencing the real Misty, not the professional facade at the studio. This was not a pretty person, however attractive the packaging. Shallow, self-absorbed airhead came to mind.

It was clear that Misty had sought me out to exact revenge on Becky and the show. When she turned to gossip about the VCs, I tuned back in and picked up some interesting tidbits.

Each VC had a role on the show, and on-the-air persona. Rex had been Mr. Perfect, supremely self-assured, haughty, and callously nasty to everyone. He was also unquestionably in charge.

Doreen Sheehan was the tough-minded woman with a soft spot for other women starting family-oriented businesses. She was often a foil for Rex's barbs about investing in startups that were really hobbies and could not scale up.

Bobby Singh was the polite, supportive, techie with helpful suggestions for entrepreneurs and a penchant for investing in companies that could benefit from his staff of online marketing experts.

Dusty Brown was the business-to-business software guru, who favored sales over marketing and was attracted to entrepreneurs with aggressive sales pitches.

Storm Crusher was the loud, slogan-shouting, bull in a china shop, who either loved an idea and the people touting it, or hated them. He was constantly in verbal conflict with Rex, usually taking the opposite position on the wisdom of investing in a deal and nearly anything else that came up on the show.

According to Misty, except for her beloved Rex, whose unpleasant traits she somehow viewed as part of his seductive charm, the off-screen personalities were a bit different.

Doreen Sheehan was a stuck-up bitch. Bobby Singh was polite and unassertive. Dusty Brown was a ball-buster, keen on keeping men in their place.

Of them all, Storm Crusher was the most consistent, on or off the air. He was shrewd and calculating, used his physical size and booming voice to intimidate people, and wanted everything as straightforward as possible. He wanted his questions answered in simple sentences, preferably one, and you had better get right to the point, his point, or you would swiftly feel his wrath. He also got along no better with Rex off camera than on. According to Misty, it was no act; they loathed each other.

I was not sure how any of this was useful, but I jotted down a lot of notes.

By the time she left that afternoon, I'd had my fill of Misty Morning.

* * *

I found the announcement online. It read like Storm Crusher had been coaxed into taking over the show. He was quoted as saying, "It's important that we keep acting as a catalyst for the American Dream." That did not sound at all like Storm Crusher. It was probably written by a publicist. Crusher's sentences were rarely that long. He was more likely to bellow, "Entrepreneurs! Entrepreneurs!" I wondered if he might be heading for the same sorry fate as befell Arnold Schwarzenegger when he took over *Celebrity Apprentice* from Donald Trump and the show tanked.

I called Sylvia Sanchez and told her about my fruitless review of the building security and TV camera videos. Then I dropped the bomb about the secret studio security cameras. She agreed to subpoena their recordings.

I also told her about Storm Crusher becoming the host of *Venture Capital Pie*. "I got the impression, from Misty's babbling, that he wasn't at all interested in running the show, like Rex had. Crusher just wanted to be the star. He was after the attention, and maybe the opportunity to one-up Rex."

"Another suspect," Sylvia said.

I told her about Becky Tahara becoming executive producer.

"Also a suspect," Sylvia said.

Another PI rule: He who benefits is a suspect.

* * *

Dargo was in his car in Sacramento, trying to decide if he should look for a motel or head out of the city, when the call came in from the Boss.

"We got a problem." The Boss always launched right into the heart of the matter. No hello, how are you, nice work with that lab fire. Nothing remotely like small talk.

Dargo liked problems. His job was to fix them. The more problems, the better his reward—just as long as he had not created them. "Tell me, Boss."

One thing you had to say, the Boss was always clear and to the point. When the unexpected security video situation was explained, Dargo had just one question.

"I can use Tahara?"

"Of course. That's how I know about it, she contacted me when they were served with a subpoena."

"Okay, I'm on it. I wrapped up that other thing here. The tenant now has a clearer understanding of reality. He'll vacate on time, no more problems. I'll leave right away. Should be in Campbell in a couple of hours."

The Boss never said what Dargo should do about this new problem, any more than he asked how Dargo had persuaded the recalcitrant tenant. He didn't care, as long as it was handled, with no blowback.

It's what Dargo was all about.

Chapter 22

"You have found Isidora."

Navarro Varga was not asking a question in his eerily soft, calm voice. He had once more arrived unbidden and unannounced. As he sat in my office across my desk from me, with Tattoo Man once more leaning against the door with his beefy arms folded menacingly across his broad chest, I was grateful for my response. I was also grateful for the panic button under my desk.

"I know where she is," I said.

"Good. You will take me to her."

Again, not a question. "Now?"

"Not now. Tell me, what is your Snapchat user name."

Of course, Snapchat, so the messages would self-destruct. "BrinkPI." I spelled it out.

"Good. I will text you with Snapchat tomorrow morning. You will follow my instructions. No games, Mr. Brink. No police, no wires. You come alone. You understand what is at stake here?"

"I understand."

With that, he got up and they left. I had not needed to summon help with my panic button.

* * *

Varga had not asked where Isidora Ramirez was, just if I knew her location. He didn't know if she was nearby or on another continent. Which meant he was prepared to go wherever she might be, and haul me along with him.

The time dragged. There was little I could do to prepare. I was unable to concentrate, unable to find anything to distract myself with, unable to eat. I finally fell asleep well after midnight, but I awoke at the crack of dawn, feeling even more tired than when I went to bed.

In the morning, I chose to wait in my office. In case Varga was having me watched, I wanted to keep his thugs away from our home, away from my parents. I had not eaten much, had no appetite and my stomach was a mess. When my phone chimed with its Snapchat ringtone just before ten o'clock, I was almost thankful.

Walk to community center parking lot
Go to electrical vehicle charging station
Accept ride from woman in black Tesla
Now

I replied, **OK**

Moments later, after emptying my bladder, I was headed west on Campbell Avenue towards the Mission Revival style buildings, with their white stucco walls and red tile roofs, that had been Campbell High School before I was born and was now a sprawling, multi-use community center. I crossed Winchester Boulevard and cut across the lawn into a vast parking lot adjacent to acres of soccer fields. Saturday soccer games for kids of all ages were going strong. The activity was frenetic, with whoops from little boys and girls right up to athletic looking teenagers, all in brightly colored team shirts and shorts. The shouts of parents on the sidelines maintained a fever pitch. The parking lot was packed. It was an energetic madhouse.

The EV charging stations weren't hard to find. They were at the end of what appeared to be the only two empty parking spaces, and had good signage. I'd jogged past many times and just never noticed them before.

I stood between the two chargers, scanning the parking lot for a black Tesla. Several cars drove past, their drivers searching for a parking spot. Twice, cars pulled into the empty spaces, then realized they were for EV charging only and backed out.

After ten futile minutes, I checked my phone for the umpteenth time in case I missed the Snapchat tone, when a message came in.

Walk north to sidewalk between buildings
Turn right
Look for man with red and black football

It took just a few seconds to get to the walkway between the buildings. Standing about 20 feet from me was Tattoo Man, looking athletic and non-threating in a red and black soccer uniform, holding a red and black soccer ball. He smiled at me and gave a friendly little wave, as if we were buddies, then gestured for me to come to him.

When I reached him, he said something to me in Spanish. I looked at him blankly. He smiled and switched to English. "Turn off your phone."

I did. He extended his hand, palm up. I put my phone in it.

"Follow me."

I did. We passed a covered trash can. He nonchalantly

dropped the phone into it. We entered a men's room. We were alone. He expertly and rapidly patted me down.

"Come."

We exited the restroom and walked away from the soccer fields, towards the continuation of the parking lot on the other side of the buildings. We walked through the lot to Winchester Boulevard and stopped on the sidewalk. A black Escalade with darkly tinted windows pulled to the curb. Tattoo Man opened the back door and motioned for me to get inside. I did. He got into the front passenger seat and the Escalade rolled into traffic.

Next to me was Navarro Varga.

He spoke to me in Spanish. I looked back quizzically. Then, in English, "You better fasten your seatbelt, Mr. Accidental."

I did.

"Now, tell me where to find Isabella Ramirez."

Chapter 23

I told Varga where Isidora was holed up. He smiled and spoke rapidly in Spanish. The men in front laughed. The driver, a slight man with a prominent scar that ran from just under his right eye, down his cheek, then curled under his jaw, programmed the address into the GPS system and it started navigating.

The audio system was playing classical. "While we drive," Varga said softly, "I wish to listen to my music."

In other words, he was telling me to keep quiet, which was fine by me. We were soon on the freeway, and I considered what I had learned about my host.

Navarro Varga owned Pottery Mexico. They manufactured and exported clay Mexican garden pots from Tijuana. He had a small warehouse in an industrial area adjacent to San Jose International Airport. The pots were trucked across the border to the warehouse, then distributed to nurseries and outdoor pottery stores. Jesus Varga, Navarro's not-too-bright younger brother, ran the San Jose end of the operation before he was deported.

It was not much of an operation. When a truckload arrived, which happened about once a month, Jesus would round up Mexican day laborers to unload the goods. He would load his old box truck and make deliveries throughout Northern California, daily in spring and summer, less frequently in the fall and winter.

I had spoken to the manager of a big garden center on Winchester Boulevard, about a mile south of my office. He told me these Mexican pots used to be very popular, but had gone out of favor because they were fragile. "It's easy to tell them from the better ones. The crappy ones are a chocolate brown color, not terra cotta, and they're thicker. Someone told me they weren't baked long enough or hot enough, something like that, which makes them prone to crack and crumble. They try to make it up with thickness. Whatever, we don't carry them." He said you mostly found them now at roadside tourist-trap pottery outlets, painted in brightly colored Mexican patterns.

I had driven to the warehouse, walked around, spoken to neighboring businesses. The place was made of corrugated metal gone to rust, with small, yellowed windows, many of which were broken, and surrounded by crumbling blacktop with hardy weeds poking up all over. It looked abandoned. Not exactly a thriving enterprise.

Thick clay pots trucked in from just across the border. A good way to smuggle drugs. But, I had learned, the DEA had repeatedly and thoroughly searched the incoming trucks and their cargo, even x-rayed and broken up pots. They had tested the material, in case somehow the pots themselves were made of narcotics. It had all been to no avail. They had eventually given up, unable to get the slightest evidence against Pottery Mexico and its owner.

I broke out of my reverie to check our progress. We had taken 85 across the Valley to 101. We were heading south to

Gilroy, Garlic Capitol of the World.

When the season and winds were just right, I could smell the garlic and onions growing in the Gilroy area 40 miles away in Campbell. Though the Valley's suburban sprawl continued its inexorable encroachment into the South Valley, much of that region remained rural and isolated.

It was where we would find Isidora Ramirez.

As we approached the Gilroy exit, I said, "You must really want revenge against her for what happened to your brother."

"Shush!" Varga said. "This is one of Mozart's most sublime compositions."

It sounded okay, but I had to take his word for how sublime it was. I had mainly spoken to reinforce to Varga that I thought this little trip was all about revenge.

Once off the freeway, the GPS directed us onto a series of narrow, blacktop roads, past farmland intermixed with small homes and trailers on large, barren, dusty lots. Although the spring rains had stopped just a few weeks ago, what grass and weeds there were had already turned yellow-brown. It wouldn't rain again until the fall and we had gone right into an early, hot summer.

After 20 minutes or so, the GPS announced our arrival. The address painted on the post holding up an aged and empty mailbox agreed. We turned onto a packed-dirt driveway and were soon parked by a dilapidated little ranch-style house that had once probably been brown but was now approaching the dun color of the parched acreage that surrounded it. A tired little Toyota that looked at least a dozen years old dozed under the carport. A lone, brave wild oak stood gallantly in the back yard, next to a rusted-out pickup truck resting on its rims.

Varga spoke rapidly to his men, again in Spanish. Then, calmly, to me, "You will come with us. If you cause any trouble, you will be shot."

With that, Tattoo Man exited the car, opened my door, and waited for me. I noticed he held his gun, which still looked to me like a bazooka, at his side, pointing downward. We joined Scarface, who was also brandishing a weapon, and Varga, who was not, and walked across the parched ground towards the faded front door.

When we paused at the door, the only thing disturbing the bucolic silence was the sound of my heart thumping against my chest. Scarface knocked forcefully. The door opened, and Isidora Ramirez looked out at us, her expression one of abject horror.

Chapter 24

Tattoo Man shoved Isidora inside. I followed, with Varga right behind me. Varga closed the door. He had assigned Scarface sentry duty outside.

Tattoo Man quickly cleared the house. From what I could see from the tiny foyer, it looked to have three bedrooms and a bathroom down the hall to our right. I figured this by counting doors.

We went into the hot, dark, postage-stamp sized living room to our left, which had a couple of cheap plastic chairs and a beanbag chair. The bare hardwood floors were nearly worn down to raw wood, and a sheet served as a curtain for the large front window, blocking the unrelenting sun. A small flat-screen TV hung on one wall, which was covered with cheap, cracked, brown wood paneling. The living room was separated from the kitchen by a counter with three mismatched barstools. A small window high over the sink was open, but no breeze came in from the backyard to relieve the stultifying heat.

I had found it was usually easy to convince Mexicans you don't speak or understand their language. Just look at them blankly when they speak to you in Spanish, or stare off into space when they speak it to others, and they will then chatter away in Spanish in your presence under the assumption that you don't comprehend a word. I suppose that was due to experience with how Spanish-challenged gringos usually behaved. Which is how I had lured Navarro Varga into speaking freely with his men in Spanish. He presumed I had no idea what they were saying.

Varga was wrong. Growing up in my neighborhood, Spanish was spoken nearly as much as English. I understood full well what he had said to his goons in the car. For example, I had learned that, unlike his men, Varga was unarmed, lest he be caught with an unregistered weapon. Now, I listened carefully as he conversed in Spanish with Isidora, all the while acting as if I hadn't a clue.

"*Where are the others?*"

"The children are in school. My friend is at work. He is a landscaper."

"This is his house?"

"Yes."

"He is expected home when?"

"After work. Dinner time. Please, I must prepare it for him."

Varga nodded, as if pleased, and waived his hand dismissively.

"You have something that belongs to me," he nearly whispered. "I want them back."

"I do not..."

Without warning, Varga backhanded her hard across the face. He nearly knocked her off her feet.

"Enough of your betrayal! Answer me truthfully or I will turn you over to my men, who also happen to enjoy children."

Her face in her hands, Isidora was sobbing.

"I am losing patience."

She dropped her hands and seemed to gather herself.

"Just tell me what it is you want."

Varga grabbed her by the throat, nearly lifting her off the floor.

"Do not insult my intelligence. I want my diamonds, you miserable whore. The ones you stole from me, from the warehouse."

I heard a sharp crack, followed by a thud outside the door. Tattoo Man yanked the sheet off the window. Varga let go of Isidora, turned and stepped over to see what was happening. Whatever was going on out there—and I had a pretty good idea what it was—I took it as my cue. I grabbed Isidora and yanked her into the kitchen, where we ducked down and huddled low behind the counter.

There was a second rifle crack, the sound of glass breaking, and another thud, this time inside. That would be Tattoo Man. Then a man's voice through a bullhorn. "Navarro Varga, this is the FBI. You are surrounded. Do not move. Stay where you are and put your hands up. If you move, we will shoot you."

I looked up from the kitchen floor and saw the barrel of a rifle poke through the open window over the sink. That would be the agent who had been hidden out back behind the old truck carcass.

I peeked up over the edge of the kitchen counter. Tattoo Man was on the floor in a fetal position. Navarro Varga was standing next to him, staring out the now missing front window.

Across the front yard, what seemed like a small army of

agents, but turned out to be about a dozen, were approaching the house. Some carried handguns and wore windbreakers emblazoned with FBI, others aimed rifles at the window and wore combat outfits, complete with helmets. The agents with rifles advanced slowly, menacingly, and clearly had Varga in their sights. Those with handguns were sprinting.

The cavalry had arrived.

Chapter 25

Kyle Rizzo had, as promised at lunch just days ago, immediately made a few calls concerning Navarro Varga. This had led to my meeting at the local office of the FBI a couple of days later.

I drove into the underground parking lot of a nondescript office building in San Jose that night. What was different was that you had to have a permit to enter the parking garage, and an armed guard was in the booth to assure compliance. I had no permit, but I did have some magic words I uttered. The guard checked my driver's license, studied my face carefully, and gave my car a thorough check, complete with the mirror-on-a-pole scan underneath. I was directed to a visitor's space, and took the elevator to the only floor that did not require key card access.

The elevator opened to a small reception area. The receptionist, a woman, patted me down, a new experience. She gave me a visitor's badge and I signed in. Before I could sit down, another woman emerged through the door off reception. She introduced herself as Special Agent Karen Kwon. She had a broad, unsmiling face, short black hair and an athletic build, and wore a black pantsuit with a white shirt open at the neck.

Agent Kwon escorted me into a small conference room

and introduced me to Special Agent in Charge Alex Greene, a trim, fit-looking black man with a touch of gray in his short hair. He, too, wore a black suit and white shirt, with a red and gray striped tie. But for his tie, the two of them made me think of *Men in Black*. They just needed dark sunglasses to complete the impression.

I had never met a genuine FBI agent before. I knew from watching TV and movies that they were all "special." As we sat at the table, Greene made it clear to me that he was even more special than most.

"This is an unusual situation, which is why I'm meeting with you. After this, your contact will be Special Agent Kwon. I'm only talking to you because Kyle Rizzo asked me to handle this personally."

Greene went on to ask for my cooperation in nailing Navarro Varga. Kyle had told him about my situation with Varga, and Greene seemed confident I would agree to his proposition. Which was certainly true, but I had one condition. I wanted to know the whole story. The truth was, to protect my family, I would have given that up in a heartbeat, but thought it was worth a shot.

"We don't do 'whole stories' very well," Greene said, "but in this case, I see no harm. You just need to keep it to yourself, or I'm afraid we'll have to hunt you down and shoot you."

His delivery was deadpan. I blanched. He grinned. "Just kidding, Mr. Brink. But do keep your mouth shut about what I'm about to tell you."

Greene gave me the broad outline and refused to answer questions, but it wasn't hard to fill in the gaps.

He gave me the rundown on Navarro Varga and Pottery

Mexico. After the DEA had reluctantly concluded that Varga was up to nothing more sinister than smuggling crappy garden pots, he had come to the attention of the FBI in connection with diamond smuggling.

Throughout West Africa, civil wars, insurgents, and warlords used locally mined raw diamonds to finance their military operations, especially to purchase munitions. The international community had banded together to block trade in these Conflict Diamonds, and the bad guys had turned to smuggling.

The feds had seen a sharp rise in this contraband on the West Coast, radiating from San Francisco. They had, over time, traced the route the diamonds took from Africa into the United States.

Brazil, only 1600 miles from the West African coast, had become the smugglers point of entry into the Americas. Diamonds are small, require no special storage conditions or handling, and are thus easily hidden. All manner of ships brought Conflict Diamonds from points along the African coast, across the South Atlantic, to Brazilian ports. From there, they were distributed throughout the Western Hemisphere.

None of that was secret. The *New York Times* had even run a story about it in the Sunday edition a couple of months ago.

The FBI had gotten onto Varga's involvement through the back door. They backtracked Conflict Diamonds from San Francisco to the Pottery Mexico warehouse. Greene would not reveal how, but implied it had been a painstaking investigation. Regardless, this led them to Varga.

Suddenly, the dots were connected. Varga had apparently graduated to money laundering after working his way up the cartel ranks. He now laundered funds for several Mexican drug cartels.

The cartels accumulated huge amounts of cash that they needed to cleanse. Varga's scheme was to smuggle the loot out of the United States into Mexico. Our nation was far more interested in what people were bringing into the country than out, Greene explained, and, though cash was bulky, the flow of it south was massive.

It was a new kind of triangular trade. Drug cash from the United States made its way to the east coast of Mexico, where it was loaded onto freighters bound for Africa. There, it was exchanged for legitimate freight and Conflict Diamonds. Next stop, Brazil.

Navarro Varga's diamonds then made their way overland across Brazil, through Columbia, Central America and Mexico, then to the Pottery Mexico warehouse in Tijuana. From there, they went to the wholesale diamond district in San Francisco, and payment from the diamond wholesalers were wired to various offshore accounts controlled by Varga. Laundering complete.

Rolling up this extensive operation from end-to-end would be a major FBI coup. There was just one missing puzzle piece.

"We're certain the diamonds are coming in with the pottery, and were working on how, when brother Jesus had a dustup with his girlfriend and was apprehended by the Accidental Hero."

I squirmed. Greene went on, "Next thing I know, Kyle Rizzo tells me about you and Navarro Varga. Varga wants you to find Isidora Ramirez for him. We of the FBI are adept at finding people, and it takes us less than a day to locate her. She hadn't gone far. Now, here's the plan..."

I knew Isidora had been afraid of being deported and separated from her kids. The feds had told her that Varga was after her, a much more serious threat. They had offered her a simple bargain. If she agreed to act as bait for Varga, she would get her green card. If not, she would be immediately deported, her kids would go into foster care here, and Varga would surely find her in Mexico.

It had not been a hard choice for Isidora Ramirez to make.

Chapter 26

"Navarro Varga, this is the FBI. You are surrounded. Do not move. Stay where you are and put your hands up. If you move, we will shoot you."

While I stared past Varga at the advancing FBI agents, he dropped to the floor, beneath the front windowsill, and, faster than I thought possible, scrabbled into the kitchen. The rifle coming through the kitchen window fired with a deafening blast, but Varga was too low and the shot missed. I was stunned and a beat slow to respond to Varga's move. Too late.

In a blur of activity, Varga stood and backed against the refrigerator, his left arm around Isidora's chest, pinning her against the front of his body. His right hand held an open switchblade across her throat. I had not seen him produce the weapon or open it.

I had been mistaken when I eavesdropped on his conversation with his men in the car; he had not said he was unarmed, he had said he had no gun. I'm not sure that it mattered, but I kicked myself for having made the wrong assumption.

The agent outside the kitchen window could not get an angle on Varga, and the window was too small for him to squeeze through. It was about to become a hostage situation and I was frozen, unsure of what to do. It turned out that doing nothing was a great choice.

Isabella's right hand flashed up, as if she were reaching over her left shoulder, then with both hands, she pulled Varga's knife hand away from her body and spun out of his grasp. Varga slid down the front of the fridge, a kitchen knife embedded deep into his left eye.

Seconds later, the house was swarming with feds, led by Agent Kwon. It was too late for Varga. The knife had penetrated his brain and death had been quick, bleeding minimal.

The plan had been for me to lead Varga into the trap. There was no landscaper friend, no one lived in the place. The entire house had been wired for sound and video. The old, cracked paneling in the living room provided great places for the tiny devices. The objective was for Isidora and me to somehow get Varga to admit the diamonds were his. That turned out to be far easier than we had imagined. Once he had said those magic words, the sniper took out Scarface and the waiting troops swarmed in.

After his death was confirmed, Varga's body was bagged and carried out. Scarface and Tattoo Man, who had been shot with tranquilizer darts, were hauled off in a van.

Isidora was badly shaken and seemed to me to be in shock, but physically okay. She gave me a weak smile and whispered, "Thank you, you are my genuine hero." Then she left the house in the company of a female agent.

After Kwon briefly interviewed me, I was taken back to the FBI office in San Jose for a thorough debriefing. It ended a couple of hours later with a thank you from Kwon, along with a stern reminder about keeping what I knew of this entire affair, not limited to my role, to myself.

* * *

Agent Kwon revealed that, the day before, the FBI had searched the Pottery Mexico warehouse. There, they discovered how the diamonds had been smuggled. They were sealed inside the thick bottom support boards of the pallets, in deep, small diameter holes drilled just big enough to contain the stones, then plugged with wood filler. The clay pots were a distraction.

The feds had not found any diamonds in the warehouse, but they had suspects in custody from the San Francisco diamond district, from whom they had confiscated uncut stones that they believed they could prove were Conflict Diamonds. They also had boatloads of evidence from the rest of the circuit, starting with the drug cash, all the way from America to Mexico to Africa to Brazil to Mexico to California. Along with what they had just recorded at the house in Gilroy, Kwon said they were confident that they had more than enough on Navarro Varga to get a conviction in Federal Court. Or would have, had he lived.

Now, with the help of Brazilian and Mexican authorities, they would have to settle for breaking up the various legs of the Navarro Varga money laundering network and rounding up as many of those involved as possible. Perhaps settle was the wrong word; it would be a huge PR win for cooperative law enforcement among the three countries, and the FBI sorely needed some good PR.

* * *

I should have slept soundly that night. I was exhausted. The threat against my parents was over. Isidora and her kids could return home, her immigration status no longer an issue. I was, she had said, a Genuine Hero. Accidental no longer.

Instead, my sleep was troubled. I had dreams I could not remember, but each time I awoke from one, I felt anxious. In the morning, I staggered out of bed, wondering what was gnawing at my subconscious.

I decided that I was just stressed out from the entire Navarro Varga ordeal. The tension had been brutal, the violence, jarring. I figured a medicinal stack of pancakes and some sausages would take care of that.

It certainly didn't hurt.

Chapter 27

Elvis Cole shared everything with Joe Pike, as did Spenser with Hawk. So, I figured I could confide in Sally, regardless of my promise to Alex Greene.

We met for dinner in my office, takeout Chinese. Over soup, hers wonton, mine hot and sour, I told Sally about my Gilroy adventure. She was relieved that the danger from Navarro Varga was behind me. She was also especially interested in how Isidora stabbed him and escaped from the hold he'd had her in.

Our soup finished, she said, "Get up and show me how it went down."

My sinuses well cleared from the soup, I stood up. Sally positioned me in front of her. She wrapped her left arm around my chest and held my letter opener across my throat with her right hand.

"Does this seem right?"

I made some minor adjustments, but I was taller than Sally and we couldn't get it right. She went across the hall and returned a moment later with a small step stool. We resumed out positions, with her standing on the stool. It was still not exactly right, but close enough.

"Pretend you have a knife in your right hand. Now, slowly try to stab it in my left eye."

I did. Even with my long arm, I immediately understood the problem.

"You see, it's hard to do it without driving the knife I'm holding into your throat. My knife isn't exactly across the front of your neck, it's angled a bit around the side. Notice how you have to sort of tilt your head up to keep it away from the blade."

Sally had us switch places. Without the stool, our height difference was about like Isidora and Navarro's.

Sally showed me how, twisting her body just right, she could pretend to stab me right in the left eye without driving the edge of the letter opener I was holding into her throat. Then she switched to real time, popping her right hand against my left eye and then falling while pulling my left forearm away from her chest, leaving me standing, clutching at air with both arms. I know she pulled the punch, but my eye still stung from the contact.

"I teach that kind of move to women all the time. Even without a knife, a good punch in the eye and the fall executed properly can get her out of his clutches and give her a second to scramble away. But make the slightest mistake and you're toast."

"Easy to learn?"

"Nope. Hard."

"And she didn't just punch; she had a knife."

"Which actually makes it harder, but more lethal. She didn't just get lucky, Joe. She's a trained, practiced fighter. And I'm not talking about martial arts, I'm talking street fighting."

Our food had gotten cool, so I put it in the microwave to reheat. Over General Tso's Chicken and pork fried rice, we talked about what Sally's revelation about Isidora might mean. I did not like the direction it took us in, but you should go where the evidence leads you.

It led me straight back to Alex Greene at the FBI.

Chapter 28

"It's going to take me a few minutes to assemble the pieces to this puzzle, so I need you to bear with me." I was back in Alex Greene's office, along with Special Agent Karen Kwon.

"This better be worth it," Greene said, sounding testy.

"It will be."

Greene gestured for me to get on with it.

I had thought through how to present this and rehearsed it in my mind obsessively. "Okay. Please tell me if I get anything wrong. To begin with, I had never heard about Varga's diamonds until the day you told me about them, right here. I had assumed Varga wanted me to find Isidora for him so he could get revenge for his brother's deportation and incarceration in Mexico. So, when Kyle spoke to you, he couldn't have mentioned diamonds. I think that means that when you decided to apprehend Isidora and use her as bait, you didn't know if she knew about them."

Greene and Kwon exchanged glances. Greene nodded affirmatively towards me.

"I bet Isidora claimed ignorance of the diamonds, that she was just a housecleaner and didn't know much about the warehouse and Jesus's business."

Again, the looks and nod.

"Then you told her about the diamonds, like you had told

me. You got Isidora and me together and laid out the plan. You assumed, correctly, that Varga would take me along to be sure I was straight with him about Isidora's location and maybe have me as a hostage if it was a trap. We worked with Agent Kwon on how to get Varga to talk about the diamonds. Once he said enough about them, you would close in. He helpfully admitted the diamonds were his right away. That's all you needed. But I didn't say a word and Isidora barely uttered any either."

"That part was easy," Kwon said.

"Too easy," I said. "But let's turn to your search of the warehouse." This got me quizzical looks from both agents. "You found the pallets with the holes exposed, but no diamonds, correct?"

"Yes," Kwon said. "I led the operation."

"Now, I assume the missing diamonds Varga was looking for were from that shipment, the last one. I also assume that, when a shipment came in, the pottery would be unloaded from the pallets right away. Then they'd immediately remove the diamonds and destroy the pallets, leaving no evidence."

Greene and Kwon exchanged much more meaningful looks this time.

"Then why were the pallets just lying around?" Kwon said.

"And who took the diamonds?" Greene said.

"You have the recording?"

"I have it set up to start where you asked me to." Kwon took a small device off Greene's desk and pressed a button.

"You have something that belongs to me. I want them back."

"I do not..."

The sound of Varga slapping Isidora across the face.

"Enough of your betrayal! Answer me truthfully or I will turn you over to my men, who also happen to enjoy children."

The sound of Isidora sobbing.

"I am losing patience."

"Just tell me what it is you want."

"Do not insult my intelligence. I want my diamonds, you miserable whore. The ones you stole from me, from the warehouse."

The crack of a rifle shot.

Kwon stopped the playback.

"That was the first mention I can remember by anyone of Isidora having something belonging to Varga. She never said she had them to you, did she? She went with the revenge for Jesus story. We all did. Varga never said anything about getting his stuff back to me, either. But it was why he wanted me to find her for him. She had taken his diamonds."

"You think she played us." Greene was not asking a question.

"I do. There's something else. While we were in the car, Varga said something to his men. It was in Spanish, which he didn't think I understood. He said, 'It's too bad. She was a good one and took care of Jesus.'"

I let that sink in a moment. "It meant nothing to me at the time, but the more I thought about it, the more likely it seemed that Isidora ran Varga's Northern California operation. I think Jesus worked for her. He wasn't smart enough to be in charge. They were also a couple. Maybe they had a relationship problem, or maybe she staged it, but she couldn't have known that Jesus would take the kids. I think she used what happened opportunistically. I also bet you never verified her housecleaning job."

Greene looked over at Kwon, who had an "oh shit" look on her face.

"There's more. Isidora knew how to use a knife and get out of Varga's grasp far better that your typical housecleaner. That's what got me onto her, it just took a while for me to figure out what was bugging me and sort out the puzzle pieces. She wasn't afraid of being deported from our sanctuary state. She was hiding from Varga, probably needed time to cash in some diamonds and really make her escape. Then you showed up, dangling a green card. Ever the opportunist, she went to Plan B."

Greene looked at me askance. "How do we know you weren't in on it with her? We only have your word for what was said in your meetings with Varga and in the car."

"Hard to prove a negative. But you've told me way too much. For whatever reason, you trust me."

"Kyle Rizzo," Greene said, nodding. "You came well recommended. But we'll be keeping an eye on you."

To Kwon, he said, "I think you better pick her up."

But Isidora Ramirez and her kids, along with the diamonds, were in the wind. This time, the FBI could not find them.

Chapter 29

I had no luck with the documents we received in response to our subpoena to Yuanxing for the ShushTek orders. I was hoping for an extra green ShushNik hidden in the orders, but not only was there none, we got a letter from their attorney stating that they had done a thorough audit to assure that all devices they had made, including the ones retained for internal use such as testing, were accounted for. It was a dead end. I needed to look elsewhere.

I stopped looking after I had located ten places within an hour's drive where I could get a ShushNik case made to order. They ranged from factories to consultants to hobbyists, and each one I spoke to gave me the names of a few others. It seemed that 3-D printing was everywhere.

When I looked for bomb makers, it was a different story. They didn't exactly advertise or have websites. No "Bombs-R-Us" storefronts. Certainly not the kind I was looking for. There were plenty of sites and videos for homebrewed explosives, but what I was looking for required much more sophisticated expertise. When I found it, I did not have to go far.

* * *

Boomer Montana was the epitome of a coot. I looked it up, it means eccentric old man. Check, check, check.

Boomer lived in a cabin in the Santa Cruz Mountains, off Bear Creek Road, between Los Gatos and Boulder Creek. He had warned me that GPS wouldn't help me, that I needed to carefully follow his directions, which used natural landmarks to navigate the nameless, hair-raising, one-lane, mountain roads that led to his place.

He was right. Once off Bear Creek Road, itself hairy, the shoulderless pavement had no straightaways, just a seemingly endless series of harrowing curves bordered by sheer drops on one side and the dense redwood forest on the other. Turns to connecting roads came at unexpected, often nearly hidden places and weird angles. His directions were to turn at the huge boulder shaped like a heart. Opposite the charred redwood split by lightening. Things like that.

The last few miles, all uphill, took nearly an hour. The speedometer never got to double digits. By the time I found my destination at the end of a narrow strip of blacktop, my heart had been in my mouth so long it felt like it belonged there. I parked next to an old Ford F-150 pickup, apologized to my Prius for the ordeal, and followed the sound of electric hand tools to a large barn about 100 feet behind the cabin.

Boomer Montana looked so much like Willie Nelson, I had to resist looking around for a guitar. He had stopped whatever he was doing inside and greeted me just outside the barn.

"I'm Joe Bing," I said.

"'Course you are. No one gets here by accident. Let's go sit on the porch."

The porch ran along the back side of the cabin, facing the

barn to the west. The tall redwoods gave us good afternoon shade. Unlike the still, dusty valley oven in Gilroy, about 20 miles away as the crow flies, the breeze off the Pacific made the mountain air feel almost crisp, and I could smell the forest and heard a symphony of birds proclaiming their joy at being alive.

I sat on an old wicker chair. Boomer Montana went inside and was back in a minute with a couple of cold cans of beer. He hadn't asked, and I'm not much of a beer drinker, but I sensed that this afternoon, I would be.

"First things first," he said, after he sat next to me in a similar chair and took a slug of beer. "I got nothing to do with those two quarterbacks."

Meaning Boomer Esiason and Joe Montana. "You must be sick of being asked that," I said.

"You have no idea. Best to just get it out of the way. Real name's Edgar, but got the nickname Boomer working explosives in 'Nam and it stuck."

"Did you cause them or prevent them?"

"Little of both. Lot of places. Twenty years and out."

"Army?"

"You bet. You?"

"College boy. No military."

"Won't hold it against you. Different times."

We both drank some beer.

"Curt Kowalski says you're okay," Boomer said.

I nodded.

"Tell me about your case."

I told him about the exploding ShushNik.

"Cone of silence, huh? I bet they got the idea from *Dune*. Read that in 'Nam."

I was glad I had done my homework and read the science fiction novel after I had googled "cone of silence" when I first took the case.

"They used the same idea on *Get Smart*. Watched that when I was a kid. Damn thing never worked right. Don Adams cracked me up, and I was in love with Agent 99."

Okay, we've bonded. "I'm trying to figure out who could have made the bomb, where they got the material." I told him how easy it was to get the case, screen, and power button. "I figure with all the IEDs, there are a lot of military types who know this stuff."

"Saw the thing go off on the show. Very precise explosion. That's the thing."

"How so?"

"Look, these days I blow things up, or help others do it. Mainly construction work, sometimes some, um, military or security consulting. Anyway, I got all these woods." He gestured to the forest. "Plenty of room and privacy to test devices. Big booms, no big deal.

"Now, your typical bomb builder isn't into precision, especially the terrorists and guerillas. The whole idea of what they do is collateral damage. The bigger the boom, the better. The only things that limit the size of their explosions are available materials and size, as in where they want to hide the thing."

"This one was very small," I said, "and, like you said, precise."

"Personal, is what it was. Just right to take out the one guy, minimal damage just a few feet away. Hard to get that right. Plastic explosives make real destructive shock waves. No, this is specialized work. Then there's the other thing."

"What's that?"

"I read the forensic lab report you sent me. They were careful not to specify the exact type of explosive, just that it was consistent with the family of plastic explosives. Granted, they had a small amount of material to work with. But they either couldn't pin it down or didn't want to. Makes me think this was designer work."

"Designer?"

"Made for the exact purpose of taking out one human being."

"Who has those skills?"

Boomer stared off into the distance, like he was seeing something out there only he could see. "Son, I'm afraid you are talking CIA and other major spook services. Stuff they've been working on for years. Exploding pens, cell phones, like that. PADs. Personal assassination devices."

* * *

Before I left the mountain, Boomer cleared up something that had been bugging me. Rex Baker and David Novak had both been injured by the blast. Boomer said that the fact that David's injuries were minor, especially compared to Rex, who had been blown apart, showed how precisely the bomb had been designed. But what puzzled me was why the other VCs were nearly unscathed, and just the one cameraman had just been knocked on his butt. No one had needed more than onsite first aid.

Boomer showed me a diagram he had made of the blast, showing the positions of the people on the set. I had emailed him the layout, including the positions of the chairs and the marks where Rex and David had stood. I got that information from the police report and had verified it the day I visited the set.

"As everyone saw, Rex was facing David when it went off," Boomer said. "He was holding it in front of his chest and looking down at it. When it detonated, his body absorbed the blast waves. You could say he took one for the team."

He had drawn lines showing the blast radiating from the device. There was a pie-shaped wedge where there were no blast lines. It encompassed the VC's chairs.

"They'd have gotten a little bit of it, but not enough to matter. I bet their injuries were from their movements when they reacted to the blast. As for the camera guy, he was close enough to get the outer scatter edge, just enough to knock him on his ass."

That had not shown up on the broadcast videos from any of the cameras, because, at the time, the center and left cameras were focused on Rex and the right camera was on David. But it accounted for the evidence of their reported bumps and bruises.

Boomer nodded appreciatively, "Like I said, it was precision design. Mighty fine work."

Chapter 30

I've been accused of clowning around, but this was the first time in my vast detective career that it was part of the job.

The Great Clownosky was a clown-magician. Sitting in my office, dressed in jeans and a blue blazer over a dress shirt, with short brown hair tinged with gray, he looked like an average guy, medium build, maybe 50 years old, the kind you wouldn't quite be able to describe if he had sat at the next table at lunch. I had read that clowns were often shy people who used the makeup and costume to hide their real selves yet draw attention. I had seen photos of The Great Clownosky performing on his website, and there he looked impressive and memorable.

"My name's Joe Brink," I said, offering my hand. His shake was weak and brief.

"Just call me Clownosky," he said.

It takes all kinds.

Clownosky was seeing me as a favor to Sally. She knew him because he had been a client. He told me about it. It seems clowns who work adult parties and corporate events can become the target of men who overdose on alcohol and testosterone, and decide it would be fun to taunt and maybe beat on the clown. He came to Sally's studio after a particularly ugly encounter put him in the hospital.

"You always have hecklers, you learn to make it part of your act, but the physical stuff is different. Happens after the act. Sally taught me how to handle myself. Drunk guys are lousy fighters, they're slow and sloppy, and now I can usually make it into a joke—on them."

If David had switched the devices, it had happened on the air. One line of defense would be to show that it could not have happened while the whole world was watching, live and in color. Sylvia was concerned about going that route because the prosecutor might produce an expert witness who could show how David could have done it. Clownosky would be our expert—if his testimony helped our case.

I showed Clownosky the footage from *VC Pie* from all three cameras. He had already reviewed the broadcast video I had emailed to him. As we watched, even in slow motion, I once more could not see how David could have made the switch. After the last video played, I said so.

"Oh, for the days before everyone could make a video recording," he said. "Used to be we wouldn't allow video recording devices at a performance, and it was easy to police. On TV, we worked out the camera angles in advance, so the director and cameramen were part of the act, protecting our secrets while we fooled the audience together. That also doesn't work anymore. Where there are people, there are video recordings. So, we magicians have had to up our game. Can't just distract people with patter and pretty assistants, or dogs or birds or flames."

Clownosky stood up. From an inside blazer pocket, he produced a blue box of playing cards.

"Just an ordinary deck of cards," I quipped.

"In this case, it actually is. About the same size as the

shush thing. Write your name on it, please."

I took a pen and did so.

"Thank you. Now, I'm dressed like your client was, right?"

"Right."

He reached behind himself and, from under the back of his blazer, whipped out a tray. I was detecting that this was no ordinary blazer. He put the tray on my desk and put the card deck on it. Then he had me roll my seat away from the desk. He picked up the tray with his left hand and stood in front of me.

"Okay, Mr. Perfect, here's yours."

Clownosky picked up the box with his right hand. He handed it to me. I took it.

"Ta-da," he said.

I was holding a red box of playing cards. The blue box was nowhere to be seen. I hadn't seen the switch, yet I could swear I was watching his right hand the whole time.

Clownosky clapped his hands and a blue box of cards appeared in his right hand. It must have come from up his sleeve, but again, I hadn't seen it. He handed it to me. My signature was there, exactly where I'd written it, complete with the extra flourish I'd added.

"How?"

"That, you don't get for free. But now, I'm afraid you know that your client could have done it. And I've probably blown my chance at a fee."

* * *

I watched all the camera videos again, focusing on David's

hands from the time he picked the tray off the table until he handed Rex Baker his green ShushNik. At no time did I spot a switch, even going frame-by-frame. Because of the camera angles, there were several times when David's body blocked my view of his hands for a couple of seconds. That could have been when it had happened. I just didn't know. And I couldn't ask him, in case he admitted something we didn't want to know.

Sylvia had been right. The "he couldn't have made the switch" defense was off the table.

Chapter 31

"There's a hearing this afternoon to resolve the security video matter," Sylvia said over the phone after I told her about my Clownosky disappointment. "Judge Norris is just as fed up as we are."

Sylvia Sanchez and I were convinced that the security video held the key to David Novak's case. Either someone else had switched the devices during that two-hour window, or David had. It should have been a simple matter to get the recordings. It was, instead, a lesson for me in the tangled webs lawyers can weave.

Sylvia had subpoenaed Rex Baker Studios, which still existed, though only as a shell with a couple of administrative employees while its affairs were being wound down. Their lawyer claimed the company knew of no such security cameras. Sylvia responded with a precise description of their locations, which Misty had provided to me, and an offer to help them locate the elusive little buggers. They declined our offer, acknowledged the cameras had magically been located and were Wi-Fi connected, but said they knew nothing about where the recordings were stored. Sylvia offered technical assistance to locate the cloud destination. She also suggested they locate the invoices. Lo and behold, they found a record of payments to a cloud storage vendor on Baker's company credit card bills.

The problem was that no one knew the password; it had apparently gone to the grave with Rex Baker. Without it, the files could not be downloaded. The cloud company refused to bypass that requirement. Sylvia went back to Judge Norris to get a court order compelling them to deliver the files. The cloud company fought the order, on the grounds that Baker had opened a personal account, so the files had belonged to him, not Rex Baker Studios. They would release the files, but only to the decedent's estate.

Sylvia dutifully subpoenaed the lawyer who was acting as executor of Baker's estate. He agreed to comply; his job was to tidy up loose ends for heirs, and viewed this one as a mere annoyance. Someone in his office sent the cloud storage company the necessary paperwork to assert the executor's rights, then went through an online "forgot your password?" ritual and downloaded the files. But before they could work out the technical details of how Sylvia wanted them transmitted to her, they got a court order from a judge in Burbank blocking release of the files. The TV network had asserted its rights to the video.

The network now owned the show, including all previous episodes. That included all recordings, which, they claimed, meant that the security videos, which included episodes of the show, were theirs. They also asserted their rights under federal copyright law.

And so, with much slow back-and-forth, that was where we stood. And our judge was fed up.

Sylvia had filled me in on Judge Laticia Norris, and I'd spent some time researching her online as well. She had been on the bench for three decades and looked like a black

Ruth Bader Ginsberg. It was rumored that she had last smiled in 2003, but there was no recorded video evidence to prove it. Decidedly liberal, reflecting the political bent of Silicon Valley, Judge Norris had had her fill of lawyers over her long career on the bench and tolerated no nonsense from them. She ran a tight courtroom, and was equally tough on prosecution and defense attorneys.

"She's an equal opportunity hardass," Sylvia said. "Which in this case may work in our favor."

Our exasperated judge had ordered today's hearing with all the parties—the production company, the estate, the network, even the cloud storage company—and their lawyers, along with the prosecutor and Sylvia.

While Sylvia explained all the legal issues and the positions of all the players in this circus, I also learned why the network had just acquired the rights to *Venture Capital Pie* instead of simply buying Rex Baker Studios. They got the asset they wanted with none of the excess baggage. The network did not have to deal with the lease, equipment, employees, tax filings, or any other obligations of the production company. That was left for Baker's estate, and his executor had hired a specialist to deal with it all, otherwise known as wrapping up its affairs, so the beneficiary of the estate, in this case Ryan Baker, would inherit the net assets and none of the headaches.

That meant "the bitch" had not fired Misty Morning. The executor was the one who had terminated every Rex Baker Studios employee. Becky Tahara had subsequently been hired by the network to run the show. Misty had not been offered a job by the network, though that was in all likelihood Becky's decision. I was certain that Misty would not appreciate the distinction.

* * *

"Judge Norris kicked ass! Her exact words were, 'This is a murder case; the copyright issue is bullshit.' She did agree that the studio owned the videos, and instructed Baker's executor to work that out with them, but only after he sends me copies of the files, which the judge made clear will happen tomorrow or she will start throwing people in jail for contempt of court. I'll send them to you as soon as I get them."

Sylvia had one other thing to discuss. It seems that our judge, who had started her legal career as a public defender, was happy to see the PD's office mounting a vigorous defense of David Novak. She was, however, dismayed when she learned that I was working *pro bono* to avoid negative publicity.

"She and my boss go back a long time," Sylvia said. "Judge Norris called her and told her, and I quote, 'I don't give a shit about negative publicity. You find a way to pay that young man.'"

"I've never met her," I said, "but I love her."

"You should. As soon as you sign up, you're on the payroll, as what we in the county system call 'extra help.' You also get expenses and a parking sticker." She told me who the administrative person was I should work with in her office to make all that happen, and warned me to pay careful attention to the time and expense reporting rules. "This is government bureaucracy, Joe. Following the rules is more important than anything else."

"Any chance of back pay?"

"Don't you wish. We public officials tend to get indicted if we try to back-date anything, however minor."

I rushed to my car, determined to get to the Public Defender's office before they closed for the day. I had important paperwork to complete. I was going to be extra help; what a fantastic concept. Income! Not to mention a county parking sticker. It was always a bitch to find a space in a county government lot.

Chapter 32

I found the PopSwap on an online magician supply website. It cost me $300 with free 2-day shipping. Sylvia said I'd get reimbursed for that.

PopSwap was one of several similar mechanical devices available that all pretty much did the same thing. You strapped it onto your arm. It was initially set up to swap playing cards. You loaded it with card A and held card B in your hand just so. Then you jerked your arm a little and, in a flash, card A was fired into your hand and card B was withdrawn up your arm.

Even with a helpful YouTube video, it had taken me hours to learn to use PopSwap well enough to get it to work correctly about half the time. You had to hold card B in just the right position. You had to twitch your arm just right to activate the swap. You had to pinch card A as the swap occurred. Not easy.

I never got the thing to work with a sport coat on, even one with very loose sleeves, but, with Sally's assistance, I managed to learn how to adjust it to handle other objects. I used two smartphones to simulate the ShushNik and the bomb. It was a lot harder than with playing cards. But it worked.

Now I could demonstrate at least one way the ShushNik

could have been surreptitiously swapped for the bomb in front of people without them realizing it. There was no need to pay Clownosky to do it. Sylvia said she still might call him as an expert witness, especially since I was still so klutzy with it.

I pointed out that if I could learn to do it, Hudson or David could have, and the killer would have been motivated to perfect the skill. Sylvia said she'd take that notion under advisement. Was that a polite way of blowing me off? I couldn't be sure. She was, after all, a lawyer.

* * *

Dargo was back in Campbell, keeping an eye on Brink. He had again placed the call from the pedestrian bridge over San Tomas Expressway. He decided to try good news, bad news. "Tahara got the studio all hot over their ownership and the copyright thing. Then the judge in Burbank, who has certain personal habits he does not want made public, issued the injunction."

The Boss snapped, "That's it?"

"Today, the judge up here said, 'Screw the copyright; screw your ownership, give up the damn videos.' The defense will have them tomorrow."

"You couldn't get to him?"

This was not the time to correct the Boss about the judge's gender. "This judge is real old, been on the bench forever, and doesn't give a shit anymore about reputation or money. And I didn't think you'd want me to threaten this judge's family."

"No, you were right about that. It would be too risky,

we'd expose too much."

Dargo decided to shut up and give the Boss time to think. After a moment, the Boss said, "The whole issue with those goddamn videos is that they might show Ambrose making the switch."

"If they do, the chain goes from Ambrose to Tahara," Dargo said. "Then to you."

"Time to cut the chain," the Boss said.

Dargo had an idea he'd been noodling on that would do just that. That was part of his job, developing contingency plans for various scenarios. This one he wanted to run by the Boss. It didn't take long, because the Boss only wanted the headlines, no details. It was like giving a report using Twitter.

"What a fuckup," the Boss said when Dargo was done. "I thought you said it was in the bag. The patsy has a public defender and a greenhorn PI, and they caused this shit? And you couldn't stop it?"

Dargo kept quiet, once more thankful for their physical distance from each other.

"Okay, I like it. It tidies up loose ends. But no more screw-ups," the Boss said, ending the call.

Too bad, Dargo thought, that they had already given Tahara the million bucks she'd used to buy her condo in Burbank. At least they wouldn't be paying Ambrose the Boss's million dollars they owed him for his part of the job. They'd held off on that payment as insurance that Ambrose wouldn't get cold feet and do a runner. They'd needed him to stick around to keep the frame on Novak.

Dargo knew he would need to hire some good, professional help, and fast. That would be no problem, it just took money. One of the things he liked about the Boss was he never asked how much something would cost, and never balked at the bill. Dargo would go top drawer, spend top dollar. He had to make sure this job went without a hitch.

This time, the burner phone landed nearly on the boundary between two expressway lanes. It took nearly three minutes before it was flattened by a big SUV. Dargo, ever the detail man, compulsively timed it.

As he walked away, Dargo thought about what had been nagging him for a while. The chain went from Ambrose to Tahara to him, not the Boss. Those two had only dealt with Dargo, they had no idea who the Boss was, and the Boss knew it. Best not to mention that to the Boss, but it was something to worry about. Like, maybe the last step in cutting the chain was the Boss cutting him.

Chapter 33

I was confident that this would be the day I solved the case. From the throng of people crowding the set, I would cleverly detect the culprit who had switched the ShushNik with the designer bomb and save our client. Me, Joe Brink, the Genuine Hero, would unmask the real killer.

Who would this mysterious murderer be? Who would tamper with the green ShushNik, unaware that his or her movements were being recorded? I felt like a kid waiting to be allowed to unwrap the present that surely was his new bike.

But no. The long-awaited security videos were boring. Watching them, my excitement gradually leaked away, like air escaping from a small hole in an inflatable life raft. I was sinking. I started with the middle of the three cameras. Because they were above the roof of the control room, the cameras looked a bit downward onto the set.

Becky Tahara had been blowing smoke when she said that there had been maybe 20 people milling around, doing all sorts of things on the set, especially between 5 p.m. and 7 p.m. I had written that down in my detective's notebook when she said it. It was total bullshit. She was probably just obfuscating to protect her precious show.

I started watching the video starting at 8 a.m. of that fateful day. I got to fast-forward through the scene of an empty set, the VC's chairs off to the side, until around noon, when a woman spent about a half-hour cleaning the floor. At 1:12 p.m., a guy came out and put the chairs in place, using marks on the floor to align them just so. I noticed that the seat on the center chair, Rex Baker's chair, was padded higher than the others. I saw several other marks on the floor, including one where the entrepreneurs stood, another halfway between there and the chairs, where Rex Baker had met his demise. Then more fast-forwarding with nothing changing until 4:12 p.m., when the same guy carried a small table onto the set and placed it on its mark.

At 4:48 p.m., Misty, David and Hudson walked onto the set together. David was carrying an attaché case. He placed it on the table, opened it, and put the five colored ShushNiks on the table. The three stood around the table, facing the VC's chairs. Misty gestured and pointed, apparently orienting David and Hudson to the set, the location of the control room, cameras and overhead microphones, that sort of thing. She made a wide motion with her hands and they all laughed.

Then David and Hudson picked up the devices and did the on-off test. Because of the camera angle and distance, I could not see their hands, and Misty had moved to a position that partially blocked the view. As each ShushNik came on, Hudson or David held it up so Misty could see the screen, appeared to turn it off, and put it back on the table. Misty then arranged the devices and tray on the table, and, on the dot of 5 p.m., the three walked off the set.

I watched those 12 minutes several times, in slow motion

and freeze-frame.

At 5:37 p.m., a man came out and appeared to be talking to someone in the control room as he moved around the set testing sound levels. Seemingly satisfied, he left, and nothing happened until 6:28 p.m., when a woman walked onto the set, the bright lights used for the broadcast all came on, and she appeared to use a handheld device to check lighting levels at various locations. At 6:46 p.m., the VCs made their appearance in a group, took their seats, and were fussed over by aides who made minor last-minute clothing and makeup adjustments. The VCs chatted with each other and, at precisely 7 p.m., they adjusted themselves in their seats as the show began.

After going out for a much-needed lunch break and a walk around to clear my head, I ran through the videos from the other two security cameras. They revealed nothing new.

I had my answer.

After Misty, David and Hudson left the set at 5 p.m., no one touched the devices. The sound guy and lighting gal had stood near the table, but I painstakingly watched them from all three cameras. They never came within a foot of the devices on the tabletop. The rest of the action was all on the other side of the set, by the chairs.

Hudson Ambrose had done the on-off test with the green ShushNik, the one that later exploded in the hands of Mr. Perfect. Neither he nor David had reported remembering that detail. To be more precise, it was the device that, at some point between the time he showed it to Misty at 4:57 p.m., and the time its replacement blew up in Rex Baker's hands a little over two hours later, had been exchanged for the bomb.

Misty had never touched the green ShushNik. Nor had David, after he took it out of his attaché case. The only one who could have swapped out the green ShushNik for the bomb before David started passing them out in front of millions of viewers was his partner. If so, Hudson had done it immediately after showing its working screen to Misty. The Great Clownosky had convinced me that that was indeed possible.

Much to my dismay. I had not uncovered the hidden perpetrator I had sought. Boring or not, I was certain the field had been narrowed to two not-so-hidden suspects. Since I had to assume our client's innocence, it was time to focus hard on Hudson Ambrose, who had been in plain sight since I got on the case. I was dismayed that I had not already investigated him more deeply. The videos did not reveal the switch, but it was the only possible explanation that exonerated our client. Therefore, I would proceed as if it were true.

But why would Hudson have done it? Sylvia and I had discussed someone being in cahoots with Danica Baker or Ryan Baker, or maybe both. We had recently added Storm Crusher and Becky Tahara to our list. Was Hudson an accomplice of one of them?

I was about to call Sylvia with the news and suggest we do some brainstorming, when she called me. Moments later, I closed my office and headed for hers.

Chapter 34

After parking in a space reserved for county employees, feeling smug and vastly superior to the poor peasants driving around the hopelessly full visitors section, I walked a short distance and entered the Public Defender's building. My brand-new county ID badge meant I didn't have to stop at reception. I just nodded at the security guy and strolled inside, like I owned the place.

I walked directly to Sylvia's office. She was sitting behind her desk with her back to the door, staring out her office window as I came in. Without turning around, she said, "Please close the door, Joe." She wasn't psychic. She could see my reflection in the window.

I did as asked and sat. Sylvia slowly turned around in her chair to face me. She stared at me, yet didn't seem to see me, as if lost in thought.

When the silence became uncomfortable, I said. "What is it?"

She shook her head and came out of her trance. "You never know what other people's lives are like, do you?"

That seemed rhetorical, so I said nothing.

Sylvia sighed. "I called you right after a rather lengthy conference with the judge and prosecutor, along with Scott Fortunato, a lawyer representing Ryan and Danica Baker. I had sent the Bakers notice that I wanted to depose them. Their lawyer suggested we have this meeting with the judge first."

She stared off again. Then refocused on me. "It seems we got it wrong about the Baker family."

"How so?"

"Danica Baker is bipolar and schizophrenic."

I was stunned. I had not detected a hint of that.

"According to rather extensive medical records I was permitted to review, her condition did not become apparent until a few years after her marriage, by which time, she was a mother. Which, by the way, is why the Baker's had not had more children. They were worried about the illness being inherited.

"Anyway, her manic episodes became more frequent. She would disappear, only to call Rex from a Vegas hotel, where she'd had promiscuous sex, gambled, drank, and who knows what all. She would just sort of snap out of it, but have no memory of what had happened, how she'd gotten there, or who she'd been with.

"Rex got her into treatment, but then the delusions started to emerge. When she was delusional, she thought Rex was part of a plot to control her mind and steal her son and money. He was appointed her conservator and she was hospitalized several times before they got the medication right."

"The woman I met seemed so normal," I said. "More than normal; intelligent and charming."

"It seems that now, she mainly is the woman you met. But when the delusions break through, as they can without warning, she stops her meds and has a break with reality.

They call it decompensating. When that happens, she needs to spend some time at a private psych facility to get back to what, for her, is normal. Which is where she was when Rex died, and why she didn't come back for a while."

"Does she know about her illness?"

"When she's not having an episode, yes. There's been a conspiracy among the three of them, now two of them, to keep it to themselves. They have a good act they present to the rest of the world to explain odd goings on."

"That explains the Virgin Piña Coladas," I said. "Alcohol and psychoactive drugs don't mix well."

Sylvia looked understandably puzzled. I explained.

"In any case," she said, "Rex watched Ryan like a hawk as he grew up. He's shown no signs of the disease, and has been seeing a psychiatrist preventively since his teens. When he graduated from college and still had a clean bill of health, they went to court, and Ryan replaced Rex as his mother's conservator. According to their attorney, Rex wanted Ryan to take over while he was still around to give his son advice and guidance."

"And criticism," I said, thinking of what Gavin Smart had told me.

Sylvia shrugged. "Ryan is conservator of person and estate. That means he can have Danica hospitalized and get treatment as well as control her money. And he has to report on her finances to the probate court. He's actually done a good job preserving her fortune, Joe. She's far from broke; she'll be more than comfortable for the rest of her life. Ryan also has to charge reasonable fees for his services and report them to the court. He's been expensive, but not beyond reason. There just does not seem to be any financial motive for either of them."

"I can see why Rex left everything to Ryan," I said.

"Yes. No point leaving it to her. And those servants at the estate? They're home health aides with mental health training, and she's never alone, 24/7."

I let it all sink in. "Money helps."

Sylvia nodded. "Sure, but it doesn't protect you from, what, the vicissitudes of life? God, that's such a lawyerly word, isn't it?"

"What about all the negativity about Rex? From both of them."

"Oh, Rex was a bastard and a womanizer, but he loved his wife and son. He stayed with her, and it couldn't have been easy. Their family cover story is a carefully constructed blend of truth and fiction. As for the people who they said had it in for Rex, that information is probably all good. In business, he was a tough, cold S.O.B. Not so unusual for a VC."

"I guess his womanizing was understandable," I said.

"Under the circumstances, I'd give him a pass."

"And the arguments Gavin Smart overheard?"

"Ryan was having difficulty with health aide turnover." Sylvia glanced at a legal pad on her desk. "They went through some bad apples before they found the two they have now. Rex was not patient with him through the process."

I thought about what Smart had said he had heard. It could fit this interpretation. Due diligence could have referred to checking out the failed hires more thoroughly. "There seems to be an answer for everything. But it doesn't mean one or both of them weren't involved in Rex's murder."

"You could argue that Danica was nuts enough, what with paranoid delusions. But, other than a single credit card with a low credit limit, she has no access to money and is under observation 24/7."

"What about Ryan?" I said. "He still inherits it all, and it's a bundle. We're talking hundreds of millions. He no longer has to live off his parents and some conservator's fees. Seems like ample motive to me."

"He's not mentally ill and he had no reason to kill his father. Rex Baker had terminal cancer. He had maybe six months to live. And Ryan knew it."

Chapter 35

Next morning, bright-eyed and bushy-tailed, I cracked the case. Clichés, I know, but it was a cliché kind of day.

The previous evening, I had remembered that I wanted to verify what Boomer had told me about how the other VCs had probably gotten injured from their reactions to the explosion rather than the blast itself. None of the broadcast cameras had been on them at the time, but the stage-right security video would have captured them. It was just another detail to pin down, and I did not expect much to come of the effort. But pinning down details is a lot of what I do for a living.

First thing on arriving at the office in the morning, I cued up the stage-right security video. Sure enough, when the bomb went off, each of the other four VCs did a futile version of duck-and-cover and ended up on the floor. Futile, because by the time they reacted, any blast wave was past them. But it was a natural reaction.

I was about to move onto something else when something made me decide to watch the video again, this time in slow motion. That's when I spotted it. Storm Crusher dove to the floor and towards the center chair several frames before the others. He landed curled in a fetal position with his back to Rex. *Was this the smoking gun?* Score me another cliché, and the day was still young.

After positioning the video from the middle camera, I went frame-by-frame to get the exact time Rex Baker pressed the power button. It was impossible to isolate the exact frame, and thus the exact time when Rex pressed the button, but it looked like Crusher took off on his dive pretty much simultaneously with Rex's action. It was a few frames later before any of the others moved. The whole period in question was less than a second, but one thing was clear: either Storm Crusher had world-class reflexes, or he knew what was coming.

I believed that I had identified Hudson Ambrose's accomplice. We had reasonable doubt nailed. Crusher had a long-running feud with Baker that was more than mere acting for the benefit of *VC Pie*. With Baker gone, he now had the starring role on the show. We had means, motive and opportunity.

I called Sylvia and gushed my discovery. She deflated me in a heartbeat. "That's really great work, Joe. I mean it. But it still could have been David in cahoots with Crusher."

I had already thought this through. "Then where did David hide the green ShushNik? The police report says that the cops searched him right after he came to, routine procedure, just before the paramedics arrived. Whereas Hudson was the last one to touch the green device before the show began, he had been sitting in the green room since a little after 5 p.m. and was alone for about ten minutes at the end. And he was never searched. The police report also said that they searched the studio for the green ShushNik, including the green room, but that was hours later, after they figured out it must have been swapped."

"Good lawyerly arguments, Joe. But we need to connect Hudson and Storm Crusher. With evidence."

She was right. I was not done yet. I thought I had cracked the case, but I think the complete cliché is "cracked the case wide open." The "wide open" part would take more work. It was time to focus on expanding the crack that I had made.

* * *

"You didn't answer my calls or texts?"

We were sitting outside, in front of the frozen yogurt shop, where they have some benches and tables. I needed some information from Misty, so I had texted her and convinced her to meet me. I had a chocolate shake. Misty had some frappo-crappo flavor I had never heard of, in a container.

"I'm sorry, Misty. I've been awfully busy trying to help you get back at Becky."

That brought her up short. Her pout turned into a wicked little grin. "Tell me everything."

I never could figure out what women meant when they said that. What exactly constituted everything? As usual, I ignored the request, a move that had always worked before.

"I'm going to get her, don't you worry. But I need some help from you."

She blotted some dribble off her chin with a napkin. "Sure, what?"

"How much of the show was scripted?"

"We had no script. Like, you know, a reality show?"

"So, when Rex moved to the center to try his ShushNik, that was spontaneous?"

"No, silly. He always did that when there was that kind of demonstration."

"Did he know about it in advance?"

"Of course. Like, from the pitch notes?"

"What are pitch notes?"

Misty explained that she had prepared a one-page outline for each pitch on the show. The VCs got the outlines in advance, so they'd know what was coming.

"Did you keep copies?"

"On my laptop? I'll email you the one for ShushTek?"

No need to subpoena the notes, no tipping our hand to anyone. "That would be great. Another thing. How come David made the pitch on the air without Hudson?"

"They said they had tried it both ways, but Hudson became tongue-tied. Like, he's not good in front of an audience? They were afraid he'd freeze on TV?"

Convenient. "You said you and Becky talked Rex into putting ShushTek on the show."

She ate a smidgen of yogurt and nodded.

"How much did Becky push for it?"

"Oh, lots. But, of course, the bitch never disclosed her conflict."

"What conflict?"

"You know, like, she went to high school with Hudson Ambrose? They went to the prom together?"

Whoa! "How did you know if she didn't disclose it?"

"Like, a photo on Facebook? I found it after?"

Pitch notes. Hudson Ambrose an old flame of Becky Tahara. What else does Misty know that I'm too green to know to ask about? Which led me to try, "Do you remember when exactly you started seeing Rex?"

She sure did. I had to listen to 20 minutes of mind numbing details. But my hunch had been right. They had started in together a few weeks before ShushTek applied to be on the show.

I was looking for the Storm Crusher connection, but Misty had served up Becky Tahara instead, with a direct connection to Hudson. Of course, she was obsessed with getting revenge against Becky, but it was looking like maybe she and Hudson and Crusher were all involved.

Except for Rex, Misty was unaware of any relationship of any kind between any of the VCs and Becky. She said that only Rex had anything more than perfunctory contact with the staff. The other VCs pretty much showed up, performed, and left.

The plot was sure thickening. And my cliché-packed day was drawing to a close.

Chapter 36

Becky Tahara was giddy, had been for days. She was getting ready to move out of what she now admitted to herself was a dump, to her condo on an upper floor in a new Burbank highrise. She was moving on up.

Most of her stuff was going to the curb. She knew scavengers, many from her own complex, would snatch up whatever wasn't going south with her almost as fast as she could lug it out there. Becky ate a late dinner and had just decided to empty her tiny living room first, then use it as a staging area to box up what she would take with her, mostly clothes. The doorbell rang. It was probably a friend or neighbor wanting to get first dibs on what she now viewed as her junk. She opened the door.

* * *

It had taken three goons. The leader went to Becky's place in East Palo Alto, subdued her, and waited in her ground floor apartment. The other two snatched Hudson Ambrose while he was heading for his car in the underground garage at his gym.

They dumped Ambrose in the back of a nondescript van, bound and gagged. One of them drove his car to Becky's apartment, parked about a block away, and joined his waiting accomplice inside. The other drove the van to a Walmart, where he parked in the far reaches of the lot and waited until it was good and dark before he drove to the apartment, where his buddy helped him carry in a large box with Hudson inside.

From the moment they took their victims, they kept them under control by covering their mouths with duct tape and tying them up with rope wrapped with towels to leave no marks.

If anyone had noticed them coming and going, they were just friends of Becky helping with her move. But no one paid any attention to them. It was an area where people kept to themselves behind triple-locked doors, especially after sunset.

The scene in the apartment was staged as a drug-crazed burglary gone bad, not hard to sell in this impoverished, crime-ridden neighborhood. Becky was killed before they brought Hudson in. He was unboxed and killed within a minute of entering the apartment, then his car keys were returned to his pocket. One of the men, the leader whose name was Ace, used a kitchen knife to slash the victims' throats, fast, without warning, before they knew what was happening. Hudson died in the bedroom doorway, Becky in bed, apparently just getting started on an evening of sex and booze.

Ace slashed the bodies up a bit to sell the crazed-druggy story. It was tricky to do without getting blood all over himself, and they all had to be careful not to step in the blood, but they had ample experience, and it went smoothly.

Before leaving, Ace used a small amount of vodka and a

rag to wipe the duct tape adhesive residue from the mouths of the dead bodies. They left the vodka bottle on the nightstand, along with two partially filled glasses, with the appropriate fingerprints applied from the hands of the corpses.

They guys were thugs, but they were also the best local talent money could buy. After everything was just so, they exited the apartment, closed the front door, then forced it open using a crowbar covered by one of the towels so as not to make much noise. They tossed the crowbar inside and shut the door. Hudson's box left with them, along with the rag rope, towels and their victims' wallets, stuffed in a plastic garbage bag.

They silently got into their vehicles, stripped off their latex gloves, and melted into the night.

* * *

Dargo smiled when he got the one-word text from Ace. **Done.**

He had been carefully laying down the clues that would convince the cops that the star-crossed lovers had conspired, alone, to blow up Rex Baker. Becky, the woman Rex had scorned, had rebounded to her old boyfriend Hudson. She had used sex to lure the besotted lad into carrying out her revenge. After Becky got settled in L.A., Hudson, who had made no attempt to get a job since ShushTek exploded along with their victim, would move in with her.

Dargo went so far as to bribe a salesman at an L.A. furniture store to back-date an order ostensibly for Tahara for a bedroom set designed for a couple, including her dresser, his armoire, and a king-sized bed.

He had refrained from making it too obvious. The cops would believe the story more easily if they had to work for it. He had scattered just enough breadcrumbs to lead them to the right conclusion.

Dargo was well satisfied with his work, but he knew that the Boss would only be satisfied when the cops announced that they had solved the murder of Rex Baker, closed the case, and the Boss's name was not mentioned.

Chapter 37

Sylvia called me at a little after 10 a.m. I was opening my mail, paying or delaying bills.

When I worked at Kowalski-Wu Investigations, I picked up the useful idea of hiding my home address from the world. We private investigators tend to piss people off, some of whom might want to pay you a home visit to express or redress their grievances. As soon as I got my own office, I changed my address everywhere I could think of to it. I even filled out a form at the post office. As far as the world was concerned, my office was my residence.

Or at least most of the world. It had not stopped Navarro Varga, who probably had me followed home. But it was like a lock, it would make it hard enough to find my home to discourage most people. Locks won't stop seriously motivated bad guys.

"Did you hear?"

"Hear what?"

"Our two prime suspects were found dead in bed together this morning."

Sylvia filled me in. The bodies of Becky Tahara and Hudson Ambrose had been found that morning by a couple of friends Becky had recruited to help her move stuff out of her apartment. When they got there, they found the door unlocked. Turned out that the lock was busted. When no one answered their knock, they went inside, saw the carnage and called 9-1-1.

"I have no details yet. I'm sort of at the ass-end of the information chain."

"Should I go there?"

"No point. They won't let you into the crime scene until they've finished with it," Sylvia said. "Even then, I'll have to work across jurisdictions to get permission. East Palo Alto gives us lots of business, but the cops there don't exactly love the PD's office. I'll just start working on getting the reports sent over."

I was trying to process this, wondering what it meant for our case. "What does this mean for our case?"

"Come here in an hour and we'll talk it over."

After the bill paying, which was easier than it had been for a long time now that I had income, I quickly scanned the newspaper. It didn't take long, as the *Mercury News* had continued to shrink in the face of online competition.

I may have been one of the last of my generation to read a physical newspaper every day. My peers constantly pointed out that it was always late with breaking news and you could not link to more information. Plus, it wasn't free. All of which was true, but it was a ritual I was reluctant to give up.

In the local section, the lead was about yet another body washed up on the rugged Pacific shore. This time it was a scientist who had apparently been exploring tidepools near the Pigeon Point lighthouse, just south of Half Moon Bay. As seemed to happen to someone every few months, he had apparently been swept out to sea by a rogue wave, then driven back against the rocks after he'd drowned.

In the business section, I noticed an announcement that Rex Baker Venture Partners was changing its name to DeWitt Venture Partners. No mention of Gavin Smart.

I called the company number and asked for Mr. Smart. I was told he had retired. I guessed that those two had discovered they couldn't get along without Baker to mediate. I wondered how the breakup had played out. Maybe DeWitt bought him out for enough to let Smart get out of the rat race. He was too young to just retire. I made a mental note to call him, mostly because I was curious, not because I thought it had any bearing on the case.

The thing about making a mental note when you're a PI is that you need to either act on it quickly or jot it down, or it may slip away. A good PI does not rely on his memory.

Except when he forgets that maxim.

* * *

"I've talked to my boss, and we agree. We pin Rex Baker's murder on Becky Tahara and Hudson Ambrose, and David walks. With a little luck, we get the DA to dismiss the charges before trial because our defense is so strong. With a little more luck, the cops and DA decide that those two did it and free David without our help."

Our circumstantial case was already good. I could prove Hudson was the last one to handle the green ShushNik before the show aired. I could demonstrate how the swap could be made. He was in a relationship with Becky Tahara.

Becky had been Rex Baker's lover. Rex dumps her for

Misty. At about the same time, ShushTek applies to get on *Venture Capital Pie*. They get on the show with Becky's strong support. Rex is killed. Becky comes out on top, running the show. Misty is unemployed.

"Remember I told you Misty said the guys were always perfectly prepared. I bet Becky was telling Hudson exactly what to do. I bet it was Hudson's idea to apply for the show when they did."

Sylvia nodded. "David did say they were not quite sure they'd be ready when they applied, but Hudson was confident."

"David probably doesn't remember whose idea it was originally, or how Hudson goosed the application along. They were working long hours, always together, it was probably a jumble in his mind."

"We won't ask," Sylvia said.

I understood. Better not to rely on our client's memory, or encourage him to improve it to his advantage. We agreed that I'd work on filling in some gaps in the case against Tahara and Ambrose, and Sylvia would do everything possible to stay abreast of the police investigation.

It occurred to me that I'd better take another look at my bills. I might soon be off the County payroll.

* * *

"Sounds good for your client," Sally said. She had ordered fruit with her barbecued chicken sandwich, but kept picking fries off my plate.

"I'm pretty sure he'll get off, it's just a matter of when."

"So that's good news. How shall we celebrate?"

I shrugged.

"Why do I think you aren't thrilled?" Sally said.

"What about Storm Crusher? I was homing in on him as the mastermind, but Sylvia doesn't want to hear about him anymore. He's not necessary to get David off."

"Isn't getting David off your job? Isn't it up to the cops to figure out the whole story?"

"Yes, but what if there's more to it? Sylvia said I could turn my evidence about Crusher over to the police after David is cleared."

"Well, there you are," Sally said.

I wasn't so sure. Spenser and Elvis each had a strong honor code. When they got on a case, they saw things through until some sort of justice was done. Maybe not through the legal system, but justice nonetheless. Could I just let it go like Sally said? Or did I have a need to get Rex Baker justice?

Who was I kidding? I knew I could not let it go. I also knew I could not explain why. "Maybe I just have a need to fight for truth, justice, and the American way," I said.

Sally lobbed an overdone French fry at me.

Chapter 38

I spent the afternoon catching up on what was being said online about the Perfect Murder. I'd been too busy to keep abreast of all the Internet hoo-ha.

It was too early to get much more then speculation about the connection between the Tahara-Ambrose murders and Rex Baker's. The cops were keeping the investigation under wraps and Sylvia said we should keep a low profile for a while, see how things sorted out.

What I had missed was an online tsunami of speculation about exploding smartphones. A ShushNik looked an awful lot like the current generation of smartphones, and tales of phones catching fire, often exaggeratedly referred to as explosions, were always big news. These had all been attributed to battery problems, but the new meme was all about whatever technology was in the exploding ShushNik being used in the future to create exploding devices that looked just like your phone.

The general theme was analogous to what had happened on the show. Someone could make a device that looked like your phone, only it was a bomb. They could switch it for your device and, when you later pressed the power button, ka-boom!

This was not merely the usual Internet nonsense. From

what I had learned, it was all too plausible. Thus far, the major phone manufacturers were poopooing the idea, though they couched it in glorious marketingese. I had to think they were worried sick about it.

I decided to pay another visit to Boomer Montana.

When I called him, he said that he came down to the Valley once a week or so for supplies, and tomorrow would be as good a day as any. He would save me from the harrowing trip up the mountain.

* * *

Greasy Jack's was a great place to meet if you wanted to have a private conversation in public. The acoustics sucked, what with wood floors and furnishings, a low beamed ceiling, and nothing covering the windows. The place was also family-friendly, and we had apparently run into a toddler convention, screaming kids seeking video games and lunch. You were lucky if you could hear the guy across the table from you.

When I called Boomer and told him why I wanted to meet, he readily agreed. I knew he and Curt Kowalski went back a long way. I had gotten to Boomer through Curt, who had told me I could trust Boomer completely and he could and would keep a confidence. Still, I wondered why Boomer was so willing to talk to me.

"How come you're so willing to talk to me?"

Boomer took a slug of beer to wash down his mouthful of cheeseburger and grinned. "'Cause I'm a lonely geezer looking for a free lunch and someone to spin my yarns to?"

"Why do I think not?"

"Maybe because you're as smart as Curt said you were?"

Okay, that was four questions in a row. Fun though this game was, I decided to break the pattern. "I think there's something about this case that deeply interests you. I think it has something to do with what you described as military and security consulting. I think it has to do with personal assassination devices."

"You write that down in that little book of yours, or you got a great memory?"

Boomer was still stuck in question mode. If he were an electronics device, I'd power him off and then power him back on to get him unstuck. Absent that option, I decided to shut up.

It worked. "Let's just say I know some folks who were real agitated by that ShushNik explosion. Now they've calmed down. I'm sort of curious as to why, and can't get anyone to tell me."

"I have no idea what's going on," I said. "I don't think I can help you. I was hoping you could tell me."

Boomer examined a large fried onion ring with a look of frank admiration. He stuffed it into his mouth, chewed with pleasure, took a pull of beer.

"We each got different pieces of the puzzle. I think we can help each other. But first, how come you're still on this case? What I hear, your boy is gonna walk soon."

I didn't want to get into the whole thing about Spenser and Elvis and their codes of conduct. I didn't know Boomer that well. "I want to really close the case, not just let it go away." It was the best I could come up with.

"'Cause it's the right thing to do," Boomer said. Not a question.

I nodded.

We walked to a nearby vest-pocket park, sat on an isolated bench, and talked.

* * *

Boomer was not so much interested in who killed Rex Baker as who built the explosive device. In my mind, it was all the same crime. He had a different idea.

"What if it wasn't about Rex Baker? What if it was all about demonstrating the PAD?"

Huh! I thought about that a bit, tried to get a handle on how things lined up from that angle. Boomer was patiently still while I pondered. "It sure was a great way to get exposure."

He nodded. "Yup. Seen worldwide. Showed how effective the PAD was. Quite the marketing event."

I got a weird feeling. Almost to myself, I said, "Rex was dying."

"No shit!"

"Cancer. He had maybe six months."

"Which means..."

"He might not have been a victim," I said.

"Dramatic way to commit suicide," Boomer said. "What you call going out with a bang! On the other hand, if he was a victim, and the killer knew he was dying, he might have thought he wasn't taking much away from Baker by hurrying the end along."

More silence. It was a lot to take in.

"On the other hand," Boomer said, "he may have also had

it in for Baker, or just didn't give a shit, like old Rex was collateral damage."

So much for making progress narrowing things down. Time to take another tack. "Tell me about these folks you say were so interested in the explosion."

Chapter 39

According to Boomer, right after 9/11, in the ancient world before smartphones, the CIA had a project to make fake BlackBerry cell phones that were PADs. At the time, the BlackBerry was the mobile phone of choice for politicians, business people, and anyone wanting a cool status symbol. Boomer said, with a gravelly chuckle, "It would have been a killer phone."

Making a BombBerry was hard. The devices were small and thin. The main challenge was the explosive. It would take a breakthrough to fashion a stable compound that would work reliably with the necessarily tiny detonator and battery.

In 2006, the project was on the verge of success. There were still some kinks to work out, but deployment of an assassination weapon was probably less than a year away. Then the iPhone, as Steve Jobs said, changed everything.

"The CIA had figured they could port the technology to other phones that became popular with their target audience," Boomer said, smiling at the pun. "They didn't count on anything as thin and light as the iPhone and its clones completely taking over the market. By the time the BombBerry was ready, it was obsolete."

"Couldn't they rejigger it to fit?"

"You and I might think so, but it turns out they were at the limit of the chemistry they were using. That's why you never heard about a phone PAD being used. Anyway, the project was shelved."

But I had not only heard of a smartphone-sized assassination device being used, along with millions of others, I'd seen it. I said so.

"Yup," Boomer said. "It seems that was a demo."

Boomers said that within hours, the Company—the CIA—had received an invitation to participate in an auction for the explosive technology demonstrated on *VC Pie*. There was a well-established broker, an anonymous middleman known only as Makler, who handled such transactions for all manner of items, often among parties who would not otherwise deal with each other. If necessary, Makler assured anonymity for those involved, even held funds in escrow and arranged delivery and verification of the goods—though in this case, delivery of a chemical recipe would be uncomplicated.

"I'm told the Company assumed they'd be bidding against the major intelligence services and, maybe, one or more terrorist organizations. Anyway, the bidding had just gotten to nine figures, when someone jumped to a billion dollars. Others dropped out. The Company needed White House authorization to go to that level of expenditure. They couldn't reach whoever they needed to in time, the bidding was closed, and the technology is now in the hands of an unidentified party."

My face must have shown my shock.

"Not exactly what you signed up for, huh, kid?"

Boomer had nailed it on both scores. This was all way out

of my league. And I very much felt like a kid.

"Did I mention that one of the provisions of the auction was that the winning bidder would get exclusive access to the formula? The seller guaranteed that. And, it seems, when you deal through Makler, you dare not fail to keep your word."

I had to regroup, to be sure I was not in some sort of dream. Make that nightmare. "Rex Baker was killed as part of a demo? So, the technology that killed him could be auctioned off? And someone made a billion dollars as a result?"

Boomer cracked a grin. "Less Makler's commission. But, yeah nice summary."

"So," I said, "the exploding phone stuff on the Internet isn't so crazy."

"Not crazy at all. I just haven't seen anyone call it a PAD yet."

"This could kill the smartphone companies. Unless..."

Boomer nodded and motioned with his hand for me to continue. "Unless what?"

"Unless one of them bought the formula in order to bury it."

Boomer smiled and nodded, like I was his pupil and had finally figured out a thorny math problem he'd been helping me with. "There are those who think so. Word is that a few of the big guys got together. Divided among them, it's a bargain to protect hundreds of billions annually."

"But the CIA's not sure who bought it," I said. "And maybe they hired you to find out?"

"Nah, they got lots of much better resources. They don't need an old explosives ordinance guy mucking around. Besides, trying to find out who the buyer was is fair game, and it's what they do. Spy stuff."

I thought a moment. "How can the CIA be sure the seller won't peddle it again?"

Boomer's eyes crinkled as he nodded. "Big problem. The thing is, the Company won't want to compromise their relationship with Makler, and, unlike the buyer, looking for the seller would violate the rules. Last time that happened, Makler put the violating agency in the penalty box for a couple of long, cold years."

I got it. If Boomer had a specific mission for the CIA about this, he wasn't going to tell me about it. Maybe it was informal. Maybe what Boomer did on his own was his business. That it just might help his mysterious CIA buddies would be a happy coincidence.

As if reading my mind, he said, "I'm afraid I'm just an old dog acting on his own, helping out a young pup private detective. Trying to get a little excitement into my dull life."

We made an agreement that Boomer would look into who might have made the explosive, and I would pursue the Hudson Ambrose-Becky Tahara-Storm Crusher connection. It was time for another little chat with David Novak.

Chapter 40

"What's this have to do with my case?"

David knew what had happened to Becky and Hudson, but it was clear that he had no idea what it meant to his situation. Sylvia had warned me not to get David's hopes up, that it would be cruel if our theory didn't pan out. He didn't know about the evidence we had about the two dead lovers' involvement in the murder of Rex Baker.

While I was not revealing all that I knew to our client, I also had not told Sylvia about my latest conversation with Boomer. I was pretty sure she would laugh at the bizarre PAD technology auction story and tell me to stay focused on the bits that would get our client off. That meant focusing on Becky and Hudson. Which is what I was doing.

"I can't be sure, David. How this works is that I pull at threads. Most times, nothing happens. But then you pull one and the whole ball unravels."

David shook his head and gave me his smart-ass look. "You mean you're just wandering around hoping you bump into something helpful. You have no idea what you're doing, do you?"

I decided to ignore that. "Just answer my question. Where'd you get the idea for ShushNik?"

"I was working at this startup. The CEO had a patent on

an algorithm for noise cancellation. That's important in headphones, cell phones, all sorts of communication devices. Turned out that it's a crowded field, there's a lot of technology out there. And noise cancellation is a licensing play, you can't sell it by itself, it's a feature of something else, like a phone. Our strategy to sell our stuff directly to audiophiles was wrong, our technology wasn't good enough to stand out in a crowd of established algorithms, and we failed."

"What was your job?"

"Business development. At first, I set up our website for sales to consumers and did online marketing. That went nowhere, and I started calling on the guys who built stuff that could use our technology. Licensing embedded technology to big companies is a long slog, they pinch pennies, and we didn't have the runway to stay the course. Geez, how's that for buzzwords? Mainly, we were too late to the dance, and the pretty girls were all taken."

"Then the company failed."

"Yeah, the VCs pulled the plug. They were right. But before that, I started going to some meetings for aspiring entrepreneurs. I had this idea for the cone of silence, it's sort of similar technology to noise cancellation. That's where I ran into Hudson."

"Who you already knew."

"Sort of. I mean, we were in the same year at Cal Poly, but it's a big school and we didn't hang out or anything. I'm not sure I even knew his name but, come to think about it, he seemed to know me."

"Then what?"

"Hudson liked my idea. He had great tech experience

with device hardware and software. I was the marketing guy. It seemed like a good fit."

"So, you got together."

"Yeah. I wanted to build the technology, get some good patents, and license to the smartphone companies. Hudson liked that as a long-term strategy, but he said first we needed to get their attention. I mean, we're talking Apple, Google, Samsung, like that. His idea was that we build a device to show off our technology, then either license it or get bought by one of them. I wasn't so sure, but Hudson knew how to get pretty much everything done offshore. He was right, too, we got a prototype faster and cheaper than I'd ever imagined. He was really good at that stuff."

"How'd you pay for it?"

"My mom and dad helped me out a little at first, but it was mainly Hudson who paid our bills. I got the Kickstarter campaign going, which was a big success, and we decided to try to get on *Venture Capital Pie* to attract attention and maybe get a deal."

"Whose idea was that?"

"It wasn't anyone's idea, exactly. I mean, it's just one of the things you consider if you're a startup. I had talked to some VCs and gotten brushed off, so *VC Pie* was appealing. The more we talked about, the more we figured we had nothing to lose by trying."

"How'd that go?"

"I had heard all sorts of horror stories, but the *VC Pie* people were helpful and Hudson threw himself into the process. He figured out exactly what we needed to do every step of the way. My main concern was that things were moving too fast and would we be ready? I still wonder if we were. I have no idea how that explosion happened."

I didn't want to go there. "Did you know that Hudson knew Becky Tahara?"

David shook his head and looked bleak. "When I read about that, it was a complete surprise. The whole thing with them was a total, horrible surprise. How the hell did the guy totally fool me for so long?"

* * *

I had not looked closely at ShushTek's financial statements, though I'd had them almost from the start of the case. Now when I did, I was astonished. Hudson had somehow fronted nearly $200,000 of his own money to keep the startup afloat, most of which went to outsourced prototype development.

It seemed that Judge Norris's intervention with the Public Defender on my behalf had also loosened the purse strings for expenses, because Sylvia immediately approved my request for DeepDig reports on Becky, Hudson and their respective parents, including the extra cost of expediting the reports. I told her I wanted to dot the i's and cross the t's on the case.

Hudson's parents lived an upscale lifestyle without an upscale income. His dad was a car sales guy who had hopped from dealership to dealership around the Valley over the years. His last few jobs had been for progressively cheaper vehicles, and he was currently working for a used car lot. Mrs. Ambrose was involved in several charitable organizations and had not worked for at least a decade. The couple owned a $3,000,000 home with two fat mortgages, and leased his and hers Tesla's. They owed plenty, had lousy credit and little savings.

Hudson himself drove a leased Jaguar sports coupe and there was no evidence that he had accumulated much money before joining ShushTek. So where did he get the cash to fund the startup?

Not from his old girlfriend Becky. She and her parents had a combined net worth of less than $250,000, and that was almost entirely her parents' equity in their modest San Jose condo and a couple of five digit 401(k) accounts.

It was time to follow the money.

Chapter 41

The deposits into ShushTek's account came by paper check from Hudson's personal checking account at a local bank. I needed to find out how he got the money. I was about to call Sylvia and ask her to subpoena Hudson's bank records, when I received a text from her.

Our boy goes free tonight. Watch local news at 6. Send final report when you can. Submit final time sheet and expense reports right away.

It was a few minutes before 6 p.m. As I turned on my office TV, I had to smile at the last line of Sylvia's message. The government bureaucracy must be fed, and in a timely fashion.

The local news channel went right to a breaking story, perfectly timed for the evening's live coverage.

First up was the East Palo Alto police chief, in uniform. He announced that the body of a homeless man, referred to as a "known drug addict," had been found in an abandoned warehouse in East Palo Alto, along with "drug paraphernalia." He had died from a heroin overdose. In his pockets were credit and debit cards belonging to Rebecca Tahara and Hudson Ambrose. The police had other evidence to tie him to the double-murder crime scene, and that case was now solved and closed.

Next came our politically ambitious District Attorney. It seems that, in the course of their investigation, the fine detectives from East Palo Alto had turned up evidence that linked Rebecca Tahara and Hudson Ambrose to the murder of Rex Baker. Combined with evidence obtained from David Novak's defense team, the DA had concluded that it was Mr. Ambrose, not Mr. Novak, who had switched the ShushNik for its explosive lookalike. All charges against Mr. Novak had been dropped and he was being released "even as we speak." Justice had been served by our illustrious, photogenic DA.

Which was great news. I was very happy for David. But it also meant I had no way to get at Hudson Ambrose's bank records. No case against David meant no subpoena power. The slim chance I might have had to persuade his parents to give me access was also surely gone, what with their son now branded a murderer.

I was once more foiled by events that moved faster than my investigation. Which was now supposed to be over. Which meant I was acting on my own, with the help of a wizened, reclusive old mountain man.

* * *

Cable news and the Internet jumped on the breaking Perfect Murder news like crows on roadkill. Officials were tight-lipped about motive, but an "anonymous source close to the investigation" was quoted by Fox News as saying that Becky Tahara had been having an affair with Rex Baker and cooked up the scheme to get revenge when he refused to leave his wife and dumped her. She ensnared her old beau Hudson

Ambrose as her accomplice with sex. The Internet and cable news treated this narrative as gospel. I was sure the source was Misty Morning. She had gotten her revenge and then some, and must have been thrilled.

Unsaid was how Becky and Hudson had funded this complex plot, and how they had gotten such a sophisticated explosive device. Then several new YouTube videos appeared, apparently from different sources, showing how to make a little homemade explosive device. Just what every parent wanted their curious child to see. Each specifically mentioned it was like the one seen on *Venture Capital Pie*. None packed enough punch to do more than maim any fool who tried it, and none were well enough designed to be confused with a smartphone or, for that matter, a ShushNik, but they left the impression that surely a pro could have built an exploding ShushNik.

Danica and Ryan Baker were reported to be in seclusion at their Atherton estate. Their attorney issued a string of sonorous "respect their privacy" no-comments to the seemingly famished newsies desperate to disrespect their clients' privacy. Security had been increased and the estate was buttoned up tight, though news helicopters kept flying over hoping for a glimpse of them, to what end I had absolutely no idea.

None of the news reports mentioned me and my stellar contribution. Unlike the Accidental Hero situation, it was the fate of the private investigator to nobly toil in anonymity. My mother did not buy that. One evening at home during dinner, Mom said she had been talking to some of her friends, and it was high time for me to correct the oversight.

Her son the detective needed to get the recognition he deserved. When I told her that neither Spenser nor Elvis would have sought the limelight, she looked at me in confusion. “What does Elvis Presley have to do with it? And who is this spinster?”

I looked over at my father. We made eye contact. Dad shrugged. One of us was going to have to tell Mom she needed hearing aids. Soon.

It took less than 48 hours for the world to move on to juicier news. Everyone, that is except Mom.

Chapter 42

Anna and David Novak sat side-by-side across my desk in my office. They had spoken with Sylvia, and thanked me six ways from Sunday for my help getting the evidence that led to David's exoneration. I received their accolades with the modesty that befitted my profession. Their adulation finally petered out, and we briefly settled into an awkward silence.

Anna eyed her brother in the way only a woman can nudge a man with a look like he'd been jabbed by a cattle prod. "David, isn't there something else?"

David cleared his throat and gave new depth to the word sheepish. "I guess I underestimated you. If I came across that way, I'm sorry."

Anna smiled and nodded with satisfaction. As we all rose and shook hands, her big brown eyes looked at me with what I decided must have been invitation, if not promise. But I may have been reading more there than there was; I had not been on a date in some time.

I made a mental note to call her. This was one I did not need to write down.

* * *

That evening, I made the call and got my date for the very

next day, but with the wrong Novak.

David and I were back in my office early the following morning. I brought the donuts and coffee. I thanked him for meeting with me.

"It's not like I have a lot else to do right now."

"Any plans?"

"Funny you should ask. It turns out that a couple of companies are interested in the ShushTek technology. Like I figured, they may want to integrate it into their smartphones at some point. Like Hudson figured, getting on *VC Pie* got their attention. I have some meetings next week. How's that for irony?"

I had nothing to say to that.

"I feel so foolish. I never suspected a thing. I thought I knew him."

There was nothing for me to say to that, either.

"I mean, I just don't understand. How could Hudson set me up like that? He killed someone and blamed it on me. He would have let me rot in jail."

That was my cue. "I don't have the answers, but I'd like to get the whole story, wouldn't you?"

"What do you mean?"

I ticked off the issues on my fingers. "The Becky revenge motive seems weak. The idea that she bewitched Hudson into her scheme with sex seems a bit farfetched. The explosive was very sophisticated and the plot was very complicated. And then there's the money."

"What money?"

I explained my problem with how Becky and Hudson had financed ShushTek, let alone paid for the bomb. I did not mention the Storm Crusher angle. Crusher could have easily been the source of the money, but I had not yet connected him with hard evidence. And I wanted to proceed carefully with David until I had a better handle on him.

"You think they were working for someone else?"

"I do."

David looked perplexed. "But isn't the case closed?"

I nodded. "Your case is closed."

"Then why...?"

"Wouldn't you like to know what really happened?"

"Of course."

"So would I. Want to help me?"

"Hell, yes."

* * *

The first leg of the money trail turned out to be much easier to follow than I had imagined. Hudson was one of those people who used the same password for everything, and David knew what it was. I guess when you work as closely as those two had for a year, you find out such things. Just not that your partner was all the while betraying you and framing you for murder.

Hudson Ambrose was dead, but that news had not yet made its way into the online databases we needed to access. As David and I started on our second donuts, I logged into Hudson's Gmail account. He had not set up two-factor authentication. Step one accomplished.

Using his email address and password, I logged into Hudson's bank account. Again, there was no two-step authentication. Looking at his transactions, we saw that deposits to cover his checks to ShushTek had come by wire from Bond Bank in the Caymans. From an account belonging to Hudson Ambrose. Step two accomplished.

Would our luck hold for step three? I nervously logged into bondbank.com. The website happily accepted Hudson's email address and password. Then came the screen message I anticipated with trepidation: **We have sent a code to your email account. Please enter that code to continue.**

Bond Bank required two-step authentication, or at least Hudson's account did. But he had set it up for email, not a text message to his phone. The latter would have stopped us cold, but, as David and I high-fived each other, I thanked heaven that Hudson had, for whatever reason, chosen email instead of text messaging.

The email came, I entered the numeric code, and we were in.

And there the trail ended. Each transfer Hudson had made between Bond Bank and his local checking account was preceded by a wire for the same amount into his Bond Bank account. Each of those had come from a bank named Heapank in Estonia, from an account in the name of IOM784 Ltd., which turned out to be a shell company incorporated in the Isle of Man, where the trail ended with the name and address of a lawyer who set up hundreds of shell companies with his name as the only contact of record.

From there, the trail hopscotched around the world, from country to country, bank to bank, shell company to shell company. We ultimately couldn't follow it back to the source.

Still, it was now clear that someone skilled in the machinations of moving money around the world anonymously had funded ShushTek through Hudson.

As David Novak left, looking forward to negotiations to sell ShushTek, he said, “Now you got me hooked, Joe Brink. Please find out where Hudson got that money.”

Chapter 43

I didn't think Becky Tahara's parent would want to talk to me. I was right.

But I had to try. I got as far as the Tahara's tiny front hall. From somewhere inside the small house, I could hear the muted sounds of voices. Moments after letting me in, Becky's sister, Lindsey, returned, saying that, no, her parents were not interested in speaking to the investigator who had worked on David Novak's case.

"We're in mourning, Mr. Brink. Please respect that."

"Certainly. I'm sorry for the intrusion."

I had handed Lindsey my business card by way of introduction when she answered the front doorbell. As I left and she closed the door behind me, I noticed she still held the card.

* * *

Boomer and I were doing burgers again at Greasy Jacks. I filled him in on the progress David and I had made tracing ShushTek's funding.

"Good work," he said. "I might've found something, too. Been talking to friends, and friends of friends. What you call networking."

Boomer took a long pull on his beer. "Back in the day, there were these chemists working on advanced plastic explosives. We called them the mad scientists. Anyway, one of them died recently. No big deal, guys get old, they die. Only they say he had an accident, was found bouncing against the rocks along the coast."

"I think I read about that. Near Pigeon Point?"

"Yeah. They say he was probably exploring the tidepools or something like that, what with him being a scientist. But he was a chemist."

"Maybe he was also interested in marine biology."

"Maybe. But here's the other thing. No one knows what he's been doing these last few years. He worked for a private research lab back in the day. Lab went out of business. Then he seemed to sort of disappear."

"Until he turned up dead."

Boomer nodded. "Funny timing, too."

"What was his name?"

"That's another funny thing."

"How so."

"Guy's name was Odysseus Zorba. Guys called him Odd Zorba. I met him once. Odd he was."

Back in my office, Boomer and I looked up Dr. Zorba online. About ten years ago, he dropped off the radar as far as the Internet was concerned. I finally found an address in Pescadero, a town with a population of a few hundred located south of Half Moon Bay along coastal Route 1. No phone number for Dr. Zorba in any of the usual databases.

Boomer and I agreed to take a little day trip in the morning.

* * *

We met at my office a little after 10 a.m., so Boomer avoided the worst of the rush hour traffic into Silicon Valley. I took 280 to Woodside, then Route 84 west. It soon became a narrow, winding mountain road over the Santa Cruz Mountains, but far north of where Boomer lived. Boomer's cabin was south of Silicon Valley; here, we were heading well west through the mountains. It took us an hour to cover the last 30 miles.

My GPS found the address I had for Dr. Zorba, on a narrow strip of road on the flat expanse between the mountains and the Pacific Ocean. This was rural, sparsely populated farmland. Good thing for the GPS, because the roadside mailbox was unmarked. It was also empty.

We could see an old house and barn in the distance, surrounded by acres of chaparral, behind a chain-link fence topped with razor wire. We could not see another structure in any direction.

The gate to the long driveway was locked with a chain and padlock. We could see no vehicles, animals, or any signs of life. I took my handy chain cutter out of my trunk and snipped the chain.

"Must've been vandals," Boomer said, shaking his head in disgust as he tossed the chain aside.

It did not take long to search the old farmhouse. All the doors and windows were wide open. The place was completely empty. Not a stick of furniture, no window coverings, no appliances, even the bathroom and light fixtures were gone.

"Place has been picked clean and left for critters to nest,"

Boomer said. “You catch that smell?”

“Bleach?”

“Bet they scrubbed it down good.”

“No prints, no DNA, no trace of who or what was here,” I said.

The barn had been given the same treatment. The barn-doors were wide open. The place was obviously utterly empty. I stood out front, frustrated, ready to leave, when Boomer waved me inside.

“Check this out.”

The wall was covered with some sort of newish material I didn’t recognize.

“What is it?”

“Sound baffles,” Boomer said. “Give me your keys.”

I tossed him the key to my Prius. He went out while I puzzled over the walls. I noticed the same material on the ceiling, and that the floor was concrete.

Boomer returned with a small crowbar from my handy-dandy PI toolkit. He used it to pry a chunk of the baffling off the wall. Then he tapped the underboard with the crowbar. It made an unexpected sound.

“Not a board,” I said.

“Steel,” Boomer said. “What they did was to build a steel shell inside the old barn, then covered it with sound proofing material. Bet that floor is reinforced concrete.

“Good for testing explosives,” I said.

“Wasn’t for agriculture or animal husbandry,” Boomer said.

I took some photos, then we headed into the quaint, old town of Pescadero. It means fishmonger in Spanish, which made sense; it was about a mile from the coast. It was well past lunchtime, so our first order of business was to get bowls of chili at the local tavern.

While we ate, we strategized.

"I can get more out of the locals in this one-horse town than you," Boomer said. "I'll do my rural dude, mountain-man thing. You want to handle the real estate office?"

Two hours later, I found Boomer sitting on a bench near where I'd parked my car. He looked like he belonged there among the 19th century buildings.

"Nice folks," Boomer said. "Guy who runs the general store was real helpful. Gal in the little post office thinks I'm a hoot. How'd you do?"

"The bored real estate lady seems to use her little office to babysit her daughter's toddler. She'll babble endlessly to anyone interested in local property."

"Well, I got a lot of stuff. You get that little notebook of yours ready."

We drove west to Route 1 and then up the coast a couple of miles until I found a good place to park at Pompano State Beach. Then I began writing away in my notebook as Boomer unloaded.

* * *

Dargo was in Reno when he got the call.

"Guy was here asking about the property. Said he was interested in buying some local farmland. Some bullshit about making a lot of money in tech and looking to build a country house near the ocean."

"What'd you tell him?"

"What you said. Just the stuff that's public record."

"You get a name?"

"Called himself Cole Spenser. Drives a dark gray Prius. Want the license number?"

Dargo copied down the number, but he already knew who it was.

"Anything else?"

"Yeah. He had some old dude with him. Guy was asking around about Zorba, claimed to be an old friend who just learned that his buddy had died. Called himself Boomer."

After Dargo ended the call, he decided not to tell the Boss about this hiccup. Dargo had assured him the whole thing was all wrapped up, nice and tidy. He'd finish up here today and drive to Campbell tomorrow. Then he would shut down this pesky Brink himself, once and for all. Along with this Boomer guy, whoever the hell he was.

Chapter 44

I had some insurance work to do the next day. Some guy, a plumber, slipped on a wet spot in a local supermarket and now asserted that his back injury prevented him from working. He was claiming total disability.

I had gotten pictures of the guy working in his yard, mowing the lawn, pruning trees and shrubs. In the process, I noticed bumper stickers for a couple of bowling leagues. I made a few calls and, sure enough, the guy was an ace bowler. Today he was in a tournament and I was going to record his heroics.

The doofus plumber came in second. I got great video. While I somehow didn't think he would appreciate my recording him for posterity, I knew the supermarket and its insurance company would be delighted.

It was mind-numbing work, but it paid the bills.

* * *

I got back to the office late. I'd eaten a couple of hotdogs while I watched the end of the tournament, but I had some paperwork to do for the insurance company, so I stopped in the bakery for a donut to boost my energy level. It was one of the evenings Sally had a class in her studio, so I also got her favorite cruller.

Upstairs, I let myself into my office, put the bag with the donuts on my desk, and was getting a can of soda out of the fridge when I heard my door open.

"Excuse me," the man said politely. "Are you Mr. Brink?"

He was an inch or two shorter than me, medium build, and wore jeans, a light blue windbreaker, and a dark blue baseball cap that half-covered his face.

"Can I help you?"

The part of his face I could see smiled. "I hope so." He reached into his jacket pocket and took out a small handgun. I had a flashback to Tattoo Man. Except Tattoo Man's gun was a cannon; this one was small and flat, but, I was certain, no less lethal at close range.

He motioned with the gun towards my desk. "Please, come and sit. Enjoy your donut. We're going to have a little chat."

I sat as directed, reached for the donut bag with my left hand as a distraction—Clownosky would have been proud—and hit both panic buttons under the desk with my right hand.

CLANG-CLANG-CLANG. YOUR PHOTO HAS BEEN TRANSMITTED TO THE POLICE. THE POLICE ARE ON THEIR WAY. CLANG-CLANG-CLANG.

The guy looked around in confusion as the recording repeated in an endless loop. I dropped under my desk. I heard two loud metallic thwacks, then Sally said, "Okay, Mr. Hero, you can come out now."

I got up. The recording blared. Sally was holding her equalizer, an aluminum baseball bat. My assailant lay crumpled at Sally's feet. His hat had come off. I had no idea who he was.

"I bashed his gun arm, then his head," Sally said. The guy groaned, then went quiet. Sally stood over him, out of his reach just in case, but with bat held ready to strike again if needed. "Better call 9-1-1. Tell them we need cops and an ambulance. But first, turn off that damn recording."

Instead, I grabbed a napkin out of the donut bag and picked up the gun. I put it in the fridge. Then I turned off the wonderful recording and called 9-1-1.

While we waited, I got my trusty camera and snapped some photos of the bad guy.

* * *

The magic words "intruder with gun" brought police officers within two minutes. They had to clear a path through Sally's clients, Mr. Vu, and a few people from the yogurt shop and bakery who crowded the narrow hallway.

I quickly briefed Cop One, who immediately took the gun out of the fridge and put it into an evidence bag. He also bagged and tagged the bat. Who knew they carried such big evidence bags?

Cop 2 determined that the guy on the floor was still alive. He cuffed him and called in to someone to report that the situation was contained. Then he put on plastic gloves and checked the guy's pockets. Empty. Not even car keys.

Two more cops arrived. One stayed in the hallway and asked the looky-loos to disperse, saying they'd be in the way when the paramedics arrived. The other went back downstairs to direct the paramedics and guard the street door to the staircase.

My office now contained the bad guy, two cops, Sally and me. Two paramedics arrived with their gurney and joined the party. Brink Investigation was standing-room-only, except for the guy they were putting on the gurney.

Unlike in TV cop shows, no CSI team descended, no yellow tape was strung. After the paramedics left with the man the cops referred to as the suspect, a detective arrived. He spoke to Cop One and Cop Two, the officers who had first responded. Then he told Cop Two to take Sally to her studio while he interviewed me. On her way out, I gave Sally her cruller. I sat down behind my desk and put my glazed donut on a napkin.

Detective John Rice introduced himself. As he seemed to focus more on my donut than me, Cop One returned. He had gone downstairs to tell the rest of the officers they could go. He told the detective that an impromptu party had started among Sally's clients, customers who had been in the bakery and fro-yo shop, and people off the street who had been attracted by the police cars and ambulance. My neighbors were doing a land-office business.

Cop One said that the bakery was giving free donuts and coffee to the cops, who, he said, were also getting the names and contact information of all the witnesses. Detective Rice said that taking gifts wasn't allowed, but when he was informed that they were just samples, not gifts, he smiled and asked Cop One to get him a sample jelly donut and black coffee.

* * *

"So, you're a newly minted PI?"

Detective Rice, was balding, well past 50, and looked world-weary. He had made this clever deduction after examining the date on my PI license.

I nodded.

"So, what happened here?"

I told him. It had happened fast and the telling didn't take long.

"You're sure you didn't recognize the guy?"

"Positive." I had absolutely no idea who he was.

"And he didn't say why he was here?"

"I didn't give him a chance. I thought his pointing a gun at me was enough information to act on."

"What sort of work have you been doing?"

"Mostly insurance, tracking errant spouses, process serving. I also was working for the Public Defender on the David Novak case."

David's name clearly didn't ring a bell. "The Perfect Murder," I said, "on *Venture Capital Pie*."

"That was you? The Accidental Hero?"

I smiled modestly.

"So, who have you pissed off?"

"Almost every case I have, I piss off someone, even just serving a subpoena."

He sighed, the weight of the world on his rounded shoulders. "Anyone especially pissed at you?"

"Not that I can think of."

"Mind if I look through your files?"

"Yes. You'll need a warrant for that."

Detective Rice bit off about a third of his jelly donut and nodded. I wasn't sure if he was appreciating the donut or confirming his need for a search warrant for my files, which he was unlikely to get.

We chatted some more. I kept my answers short. He seemed to run out of questions just as he ran out of donut and coffee. Then came his Columbo moment.

"Just one more thing. Why do you have this panic system?"

"I'm often here alone, as is my friend Sally. We realized we were vulnerable. So we put in a security system and panic buttons. Sort of mutual protection."

He looked skeptical. The expression fit his face comfortably. "This isn't exactly a high crime area, and you're just a couple of blocks from the police station."

"I was working on a case with the FBI. It involved a very dangerous man. I'm afraid I can't tell you more." I referred him to Alex Greene.

"Well, well. For a newbie PI, you've been a busy boy."

Detective Rice left me with Cop One while he went across the hall to get Sally's statement. Twenty minutes later, he returned and asked for a demonstration of the panic system. I told him it was extremely loud. He sent the cops off to warn everyone downstairs.

Our little demo made Detective Rice smile. It was a look that did not seem to fit his face.

Chapter 45

It had been a late night, and I had trouble falling asleep, then tossed and turned most of the night. I finally got into a deep sleep near dawn, slept late, then spent the rest of the morning reviewing my notes from our Pescadero outing and cross-checking what I could online.

Odysseus Zorba's former home, known locally as the Bently place, had been part of a much larger farm that had been in the Bently family for 150 years. Over time, the land had been sold off, until just the family home remained on 100 acres. That had been sold about ten years ago to a Nevada company named Western Land Holdings.

As its name implied, privately held Western Land Holdings owned a substantial portfolio of real estate in California, Nevada and Oregon. The ownership of Western Land Holdings was hidden behind a cloak of nominees and shell companies.

Shortly after the Western Land Holdings sale closed, the entire property was fenced, which is a hell of a lot of fence. Twenty-four-hour security patrols began, and the house and barn were remodeled. What especially got the attention of the locals was that none of the work was done by local contractors, and the security guards came from Silicon Valley. That was a 60- to 90-minute commute each way over the mountains.

As soon as the last contractor left, Zorba had moved in. He seemed to live alone and kept to himself, except for occasional trips into town for odds and ends. Like most in the area, he probably went into Half Moon Bay for most groceries and shopping. If he had domestic help, repair services, whatever, they too were not local. No one Boomer or I spoke with knew anyone who had been inside that fence.

Two days after Zorba's death, a couple of unmarked 18-wheelers arrived at the Bently place early one morning and left late in the afternoon. Apparently, these were the movers. Since then, the property seemed to have been vacant and had not been listed for sale or lease. The mail had been stopped, the utilities turned off.

I searched for relatives of Odysseus Zorba. He was never married, parents were deceased. I checked with the San Mateo County Public Administrator's office, and they were administering his estate in the absence of a will. With a little social engineering, I determined that they had found no heirs. Friendly schmoozing with a clerk at the coroner's office revealed that no one had claimed the body.

* * *

"Hello, Mr. Brink. It's Lindsey Tahara. You said to call if..." Her voice trailed off, as if she was not sure how to say why she was calling.

"Why don't we grab a cup of coffee and talk?"

Becky's sister agreed. Mid-afternoon, we met at a Starbucks near her work. Lindsey was not strikingly beautiful like her sister, but she was pleasant enough to look at and had none of Becky's sharp personality edges.

"I'm not sure where to begin, Mr. Brink." Lindsey said after we sat down at a table on the patio and I adjusted the umbrella to get the shade right.

I needed to just get her talking. "Please call me Joe."

I got a small smile. "Okay, Joe."

"You're the younger sister?"

"Yes. Three years younger."

"Other brothers and sisters?"

"No, just us."

"You two close?"

"We were very close growing up, not so much over the last few years."

I nodded sagely.

"We were always very different. Becky was competitive. When we played, she always had to win. Me, I just liked the playing, you know, the doing stuff together part."

This time, I knowingly shook my head.

"Becky was smart and pretty but, you know, difficult. Like, she had to get her way, and let you know it. I was the nice, quiet one."

Surprising myself, I asked, "How did that work out with boys?"

Lindsey laughed. She had a pleasant laugh. "The boys flocked to her, but she went through them fast. I envied her, though. I was so shy. Still am."

We both focused on our coffee a while, Lindsey avoiding eye contact.

"What they're saying? I mean, Becky was driven to succeed. I could see her having an affair with Rex Baker as a career move."

"Wouldn't you have known about it?"

She sighed sadly. "We weren't that close anymore. Now she's gone." Lindsey seemed to gather herself. "They say she got Hudson to murder Rex Baker for revenge when he dumped her? My sister? I can't believe that."

I sensed that we were almost to the point, but how to get her there? I felt that if I said the wrong thing, I could lose her. I was about to say something lame about never completely knowing another person. Fortunately, thinking it over got me to keep my mouth shut long enough for Lindsey to continue on her own.

"Okay, here's the thing. Becky had one of these fill-in-the-blanks wills you can print online. I was the named executor. Anyway, my parents inherit everything. Which we all figured wouldn't be much anyway, Becky's job didn't pay that well, but her new one would, it was her big break. But it turns out Becky owned her new condo."

Good for the Tahara's. At least they'll get her equity. Not much, she probably put down the minimum, but, to the very low-net-worth Tahara's, the money would make a difference. I was about to trot out another lame line, that it wouldn't make up for losing Becky, but changed my mind. Instead, I said, "Isn't that good news?"

"It cost a million dollars, Joe. How could she do that?"

I was slow in getting the point. Finally, the lightbulb flashed. She meant owned, as in no mortgage.

"She owned it free and clear?"

Lindsey was wide-eyed. "She paid cash. Where did she get the money? They say Rex Baker liked the ladies, and he was rich and all that, but did he shower them with money? And then dump them?"

I was thinking that he might have paid them when he dumped them to avoid sexual harassment charges, but kept that to myself as well.

Besides, I didn't believe Rex Baker was the source of the money for Becky's condo. It was Mr. Mastermind, the one Becky Tahara and Hudson Ambrose had been working for.

* * *

This time, it was almost too easy. I called the escrow agent who had handled Becky's condo sale. I got the name from Lindsey, who in turn got it from the paperwork that was part of Becky's effects. I said I was working for the Tahara family. The woman I spoke to had not heard of Becky's murder and, flustered, told me the source of the closing funds. They had been wired from an account in Becky's name at Bond Bank in the Caymans.

At my request, Lindsey called Bond Bank and said she was handling Becky's estate. She was informed that they needed a copy of the death certificate and legal paperwork identifying her as executor in order to provide any information.

Chapter 46

The excitement at my office had taken place too late to get into the next day's *Mercury-News*, which is a morning paper. So, they ran it the day after, which was today.

"Bet that helps your practice," Detective Rice said, jabbing a finger at the headline in the newspaper on my desk: *Real Hero Saves Accidental Hero.*

My building was two blocks from the police station. Rice had walked over, he said, in order to be certain the jelly donut he'd had the other night wasn't a fluke. I wasn't sure if it was the result of that taste test or the headline that had prompted his smirk. Probably both.

"Why do I think this is not a social call?"

"Because you are a great detective. Look, I need your help. Are you sure you don't have any idea who your intruder was?"

"When someone points a gun at you, it sharpens your memory, increases your motivation. But I really can't come up with anything."

He waived his hand around, as if taking in the room. "Agent Greene confirmed your story about why you got the panic system."

So now I had some credibility due to my FBI connection.

"The suspect refuses to talk, period. We've run his prints

and DNA, got nothing. Even tried facial recognition, although that's still of limited use if you're not Homeland Security."

"What's his lawyer say?"

"When I say he won't talk, I mean it. He barely cooperated with the medical staff who treated him. Refused to give any personal information. Would not talk to the Public Defender. He's been arraigned as a John Doe."

"He has the right to remain silent."

"Yeah, but this is extreme."

"Maybe his brains were scrambled."

"Yeah, that little black gal walloped him good. By the way, there won't be any charges against her for braining him and saving your ass. Anyway, along with a broken arm, the doc says he sustained a concussion and might have short-term memory loss. Hard to say, no pun intended. He can talk just fine, he talked to the doc, who said he speaks perfect English, not even an accent. He just won't talk anymore. Won't write, either. Which is a paperwork nightmare."

"If I think of anything, I'll let you know."

As he got up to leave, Detective Rice said, "Bet that article helps Sally Rocket's business." It was accompanied by another smirk.

* * *

At lunch, I told Sally about Rice's quip. "I sure hope so," she said. "Is that why your brow is so furrowed? Because he dissed you?"

"It's this case," I said. "So many people want things from me."

"That's because you won't close the case."

I started counting on my fingers. "Anna Novak and Sylvia Sanchez wanted me to get David off."

Sally grabbed a fry off my plate. "Which you did."

"Misty Morning wanted me to help her get even with Becky Tahara."

Sally snatched another fry. "Also done. Kind of weird, though."

"Boomer Montana wants me to help him find the source of the explosive."

And another fry down. "A work in progress."

"And David wants me to find out what really happened."

My French fries were gone. Sally said, "What do you want?"

"I want you to order your own fries from now on."

Sally had a point. I had done a pretty good job, and the Misty-Becky thing was just plain weird. As for the open items, they were only open because I wouldn't let go of the case.

I was liking Storm Crusher more and more as our criminal mastermind. The aggressive multibillionaire surely fit the profile. But how to connect the dots back to him?

I should have realized that there was one more item for my list. I just hadn't yet connected Detective John Rice's request for help identifying Mute Man with this case.

"I got some good news," I said. "The insurance company was so pleased with my work on the bowling plumber case they're putting me on retainer." It wasn't exactly a windfall, but it would give me a steady income stream I could count on to cover my overhead.

"So now you can afford to order double fries," Sally said.

* * *

Dargo decided he would keep his mouth shut and take his medicine.

He had stayed out of the system his whole career, used false identities with excellent IDs, each with real credit cards and bank accounts. Never filed a tax return. He routinely checked online to be sure there was nothing on the Internet about him. As best Dargo could tell, he was a ghost.

More, he was afraid the Boss would decide to cut the last link in the chain. Him.

He had gotten a little careless, a little sloppy, maybe even underestimated Joe Brink. That was something you couldn't afford in his line of work. It was probably time to retire; he had plenty of money stashed away.

Dargo, a.k.a. John Doe, was charged with possession of an unlicensed gun and brandishing a weapon. That's really all they had on him. So, he'd do a little jail time, maybe a year, no big deal. He'd use the break to plan his retirement.

Chapter 47

Boomer was in my office early. We had agreed to the meeting after we left Pescadero, to see where we were after we'd both had some time to think things over.

"Quite the little adventure," Boomer said, after I told him about Mute Man's nocturnal visit. Boomer had not yet heard about the incident; he did not exactly follow local news. "I need to meet this Sally Rocket."

"Yeah, she is something," I said.

"Curious timing, huh? Like, maybe we're shaking things up?"

That had not occurred to me. It was a duh moment, as in, *duh, of course!* Boomer had immediately seen the likely connection between Mute Man's visit and our trip to Pescadero. Joe Brink, trained, professional private investigator, had been oblivious to the obvious.

"The question is," he went on while I silently beat myself up, "exactly who are we shaking?"

"Storm Crusher is on top of my list," I said.

"Who's number two?"

"Okay, it's a short list," I said. "The problem is, you don't just start accusing one of the richest men in the world of murder. And he isn't exactly easy to investigate. He's got layer on top of layer of insulation and protection."

"I get it," Boomer said. "The superrich really are different. So, what now?"

"Now, you and I are going to put together the whole story." I felt like we had enough clues, and it was time to assemble them into a coherent whole.

Boomer grinned. "Sounds like fun."

Why was I doing this with Boomer Montana, when I had proceeded with caution with David Novak? I asked myself that more than once, and came up with no good answer other than gut instinct.

Our task was to craft a coherent, credible story. We discarded evidence that might be red herrings. On the other hand, facts that contradicted our evolving tale meant we had to change it. We had to accommodate the truth, however inconvenient.

We bounced ideas off each other, argued, laughed, ordered in lunch, and went through a dozen donuts from downstairs along with gallons of coffee and cola. By the time we had worked through our pizza dinner from MySlice, we had developed a complete narrative.

* * *

Someone we were calling Mastermind wanted to spectacularly demonstrate new personal assassination device technology. Mastermind recruited Becky and Hudson. Becky had the ability to get a company on VC Pie. *Hudson could help start a company with the right product to demo the PAD. In any case, after the successful demo that famously took Rex Baker's life and left David Novak framed for murder, Mastermind eliminated Becky and Hudson with a staged drug-crazed burglary gone wrong.*

For about a decade, Mastermind had funded explosive chemistry expert Dr. Odysseus Zorba's research in an isolated facility in Pescadero. That effort culminated in the PAD's explosive technology. After the demo, there had been a secret auction—the entire point of this complex plot—and a consortium of smartphone companies had purchased the explosive technology for a vast sum in order to bury it and protect their market. With that deal done, Mastermind eliminated Zorba with a staged drowning accident, and wiped every trace of evidence from Zorba's former home and laboratory.

When Boomer and I started sniffing around Pescadero, we triggered a tripwire of some sort. Word got back to Mastermind. That led to Mute Man's visit the other night. We figured he planned to find out what I knew, get the lowdown on Boomer, and maybe permanently silence us as he had Becky, Hudson and Zorba.

Were Mute Man and Mastermind one and the same? We didn't think so. Mastermind seemed more likely the money and brains, unlikely to get his hands dirty and expose himself like that. More likely, Mute Man was hired help. No, we were pretty sure our wicked Mastermind acted through others, from a distance.

* * *

Boomer and I were pleased with our day's work. It had been productive and fun. The story we had concocted might not be the true story, or the whole story, but it was a damn good story. We believed it and, at least for now, it was the story we would go with.

Was there enough proof to corroborate it? To us, mostly yes, with some admitted gaps to fill in. But too much was circumstantial or conjecture to get law enforcement involved. We needed to strengthen our case and, especially, spackle over those gaps.

We were wiped out, approaching brain uselessness. Boomer looked especially weary. It was time for sleep. Tomorrow, we agreed, we would decide what to do to get the rest of the evidence we needed and identify, if not expose, Mastermind.

The more I thought about it as I headed home, the weakest part or our story was Mute Man's involvement. His unannounced, threatening appearance in my office that night was a lot like Navarro Varga's, especially if Varga had chosen to come in alone. Although Mute Man did not look Latino, and the little I heard of his speech sounded like unaccented American English, it had occurred to me at the time that he might be an associate of Varga. I had not given him an opportunity to state his business before I hit the panic buttons.

For some reason, I did not want to go running to Alex Greene about a possible Mute Man-Varga connection. I had counted on Detective Rice to contact Greene to check me out, he did, and now, Greene knew about my run-in with Mute Man and would draw his own conclusions.

I could not tell Boomer any of this. The Varga business was wrapped in a blanket of FBI confidentiality. Yes, I had made an exception for Sally, but, although I trusted Boomer, our relationship did not nearly have the same depth or duration.

But I had decided to go along with Boomer on the Mute

Man thing. It fit in nicely, completing the picture, and it gave us another angle to investigate. Besides, it was just our story, Boomer's and mine. It was a strawman, and any part that did not hold up could be changed or discarded without harming anyone.

Chapter 48

The morning *Mercury-News* carried the TV station's announcement that it was discontinuing production of *Venture Capital Pie*. No new episodes would air. It was terse. No reasons were given.

The *L.A. Times* reported that, led by Storm Crusher, the surviving VCs had all pulled out of *VC Pie*. They felt the story of the show was becoming too tawdry, and no longer wanted to be associated with it. An unnamed source said the VCs wanted the show to be remembered for what it, and they, had done to promote entrepreneurship, not for explosions and murders and affairs.

My original reasons for homing in on Storm Crusher for being Mastermind of the Perfect Murder no longer looked so convincing. It no longer looked like he had done it to replace his rival, Rex Baker. And it was surely overkill purely as revenge for their bitter feud. In fact, you could argue it was overkill, period.

However, there was still Crusher's amazingly fast start hitting the deck when the bogus ShushNik exploded, and Boomer's intelligence information about the auction had added a billion reasons that could even motivate a superrich guy like Storm Crusher.

Then again, those billion reasons could stand on their

own as a motive for pretty much anyone.

I was discussing this with Sally when Boomer arrived. He looked like he'd had a rough night, his eyes looked tired, not at all the frisky Boomer I had experienced so far.

I introduced them. Boomer brightened and made a bit of a fuss about how the "little lady" had beat down Mute Man. Somehow, Sally's usual male chauvinist pig detector seemed disabled by Boomer's old-geezer charm. Later, she even told me that Boomer was a courtly gentleman; had I ever called her a little lady, she would have decked me.

Wearing a sappy grin, Sally got up to leave to teach a class when she said, "Oh, by the way, Joe, you remember Storm Crusher was a sprinter, right?"

"What?"

"Didn't I tell you when you first told me about his fast reaction to the explosion? At least I thought about telling you. Anyway, you know I ran track in college. Well, Storm Crusher and I went to the same school. He had his picture on the field house wall of fame. Way back when, he set a record in the quarter mile for us, almost made the Olympic team. He looked a lot thinner then."

With that, Sally breezed out the door. It was peculiar; Sally always walked with purpose, she never breezed.

Regardless, five minutes later I had confirmed what Sally's "oh, by the way" had made me fear. A little research online revealed that a top sprinter's reaction time to the starter's pistol was between one- and two-tenths of a second. That could account for how fast Crusher had reacted to the explosion.

I told Boomer about the *Venture Capital Pie* cancellation news. He suggested that, coupled with Sally's bombshell, it was time to let go of treating Crusher as any more likely than anyone else close to the case to be Mastermind. I had liked him for my prime suspect for quite a while, and it was hard to let go. But I knew it was time to get back to following the money.

I hadn't wanted to embarrass Boomer in front of Sally, but now asked, "Are you feeling okay? You don't look so good."

"Yeah, had a rough night. I think maybe it was something I ate. Reminded me of a time in 'Nam when we all got food poisoning. But I'll be okay."

I had the fleeting thought that somehow Mastermind might have had Boomer poisoned. Then I decided this case was starting to make me paranoid, so I let it go.

Boomer and I had agreed that, in the interest of quality control, we had a duty to continue our efforts to sample every donut type the bakery offered. He said he was a bit tired, so I went downstairs by myself to fetch the coffee and donuts. When I got back, I summarized the money trail.

Hudson had received a total of $285,000 from the IOM784 Ltd. Account at Heapank in Estonia through Bond Bank in the Caymans to fund ShushTek.

I had some new information from Lindsey Tahara. Becky's million dollars for her condo also came from IOM784 Ltd. and had followed the same route.

Mastermind had received a billion dollars from the smartphone consortium.

We had no evidence as to the source of Odysseus Zorba's income. We knew his home and lab were on property owned by Western Land Holdings.

Boomer, looking even wearier, said, "Seems we got about

as far as we can with Becky and Hudson."

He was right about that. I had spoken with Amy Wu and told her about tracing the money. Amy was not only the best hacker at Kowalski-Wu Investigations, she was reputed to be one of the best in the world. Amy said she doubted even she could get any further than I had. She said the international banking system makes tracking where money *goes* relatively easy. Once you manage to hack in, it mainly takes time and patience. No matter how convoluted the path, you follow the breadcrumbs, they ultimately lead somewhere. But someone skilled enough can make tracking money backwards, where it *came from*, much harder. She said to do that, you needed more information than I had.

"They were just pawns recruited by Mastermind anyway," I told Boomer as I dutifully took a bite of a maple log. I noticed that he hadn't yet touched a single donut.

I was about to suggest some ways we could further investigate Zorba and Western Land Holdings, when Boomer said, "Son, I'm feeling awfully hot. Mind if we crank up the A/C some?"

I looked at him more carefully. His face looked flushed and clammy, and he was clutching his stomach and grimacing. "Gut pain? Chills and fever?"

"How'd you know?"

I'd had acute appendicitis when I was in college. I had thought it was some sort of flu and suffered for two days before I went to the student health center. The nurse took one look at me and got me right over to the hospital, where I had an emergency appendectomy.

"I'm taking you to the hospital."

* * *

The man known variously as Boss, Patron and, unbeknownst to him, Mastermind, was sipping a margarita on his yacht, somewhere off the California coast, trying to decide how worried he should be. He had not heard from or been able to reach Dargo for several days now.

The PAD deal had been wrapped up nicely. He had $500 million from the auction tucked away. The other $500 million was in an escrow account, where it would be released at the rate of $50 million a year, as long as what he thought of as the Zorba formula was revealed only to the winning bidder.

There was no problem there. He had no intention of violating that agreement. Yes, $50 million a year would be a nice annuity stream, especially since it was completely hidden from the tax man. And you did not screw around with any part of a deal brokered by Makler, not if you wanted to live, which Mastermind keenly favored.

Dargo had been taking care of another little matter for him in Los Angeles when he had gone silent. This was unlike Dargo, who was punctual to a fault about checking in and had never been unreachable.

Mastermind decided it was indeed time for him to be worried. But what should he do with his concerns? This was precisely the sort of thing he would always turn to Dargo to handle. He didn't have anyone else quite like Dargo he could rely on for such matters.

He saw now that this lack of backup was a serious oversight. What if something had happened to Dargo? How would he replace him? It was his experience that Dargos were hard to find.

Worst of all, what if Dargo had gone off the reservation? He could bring everything crashing down.

Dargo the problem solver had become a problem to be solved.

Chapter 49

Things moved fast when we got to the ER. When I left Boomer, they were prepping him for an emergency appendectomy. They told me he wouldn't be having any visitors until tomorrow.

By the time I saw Boomer next morning, he was his chipper old self again. The nurse told me that they would probably keep "a man of his age" at least two more days, but he was doing fine.

* * *

Although I had been reimbursed by the Public Defender's office, I had used my own DeepDig account for the David Novak case. That was so I could earn Frequent Digger points. I had enough to get one free in-depth report. I decided to use it for Odysseus Zorba.

It would take a couple of days to get the Zorba DeepDig. While I waited for that, I had some research to do. I started with a call to Kyle Rizzo, my old mentor from Kowalski-Wu. I asked Kyle if he knew someone familiar with the financial workings of big tech companies who might be willing to educate a newbie PI and all-around good guy. Kyle asked who that fine fellow was.

* * *

Nick Marchetti was chief financial officer for a tech startup called Global Lunar Electrical Energy. GLEE was tech mogul Mike Gold's baby. He had this farfetched plan to power the world with solar energy beamed from the Moon. But this was Silicon Valley, where bold dreams sometimes became reality. After all, this was, or at least had been, home to *Venture Capital Pie*, showcase for the American Dream. So why not?

It didn't take me long online to discover that Marchetti was an interesting character. In the 1990s, he had been the financial brains behind Barry Samson's tech powerhouse, Forward Data Systems. Then he had a falling-out with Samson, who had become one of the richest men in the world. Marchetti left Forward and made it big as a venture capitalist, but disappeared after the FBI labelled him a person of interest in Samson's murder. Several years later, Marchetti resurfaced, was somehow cleared by the feds, and now he was CFO for this Mike Gold startup.

I also learned that Nick Marchetti was the nephew of the late New York Mafia boss Vito Cangelosi. I had the impression that there was some sort of mob connection in Kyle Rizzo's family as well, and he too was from New York. It made me wonder. Still, a source is a source. Especially a free one.

I met Marchetti at his office on the top floor of a two-story building in a small office park in Los Gatos, just a few minutes' drive from my office in Campbell. He had a corner office with a pleasant view of lush woods.

Marchetti looked like the stereotypical handsome Italian of the Al Pacino in *The Godfather* variety, trim, swarthy, with straight dark hair and intense brown eyes. He greeted me warmly, with a firm but not challenging handshake.

"Kyle says you're a good guy," he said, with a slight New York accent. "He's usually right about such things."

It was an interesting way to sort of compliment me but put me on the defensive, as in, don't be an asshole and prove Kyle wrong.

I was about to serve up my own left-handed compliment cum guilt trip. "Thanks for seeing me on such short notice, Mr. Marchetti. Kyle said if I tell you something in confidence, you'll keep it to yourself."

Marchetti's smile reached his eyes. "Then I guess I better. Don't want to let Kyle down. Please, take a seat and call me Nick."

I sat across from him at his desk. I didn't think it would be wise to take up his time with small talk. "Okay, Nick. I want to give you a hypothetical situation. Suppose a few big public companies got together to pay a billion dollars for exclusive rights to an invention. These companies are competitors, but it's in all their interests to keep this thing off the market, to bury it."

"Interesting," he said.

"They also want to keep the whole thing secret. The invention and the payment."

Nick smiled. "Of course they do."

"So how could they pull it off?"

"I'm going to grab a Diet Coke. You want something?"

"I'll have the same."

Nick opened his credenza, which had a small refrigerator

inside, and took out two cans of soda. We both popped our Cokes and took a swig. He nodded, as if he'd had enough time to think through my question.

"It would be no problem to deep-six the intellectual property. The issue, as you probably already surmised, is the money. As a public company subject to audit and SEC scrutiny, you couldn't just hide a few hundred million dollars of expense."

I had checked smartphone sales, and at least two of the companies that were probably in the smartphone consortium that won the PAD auction were based overseas, thus not subject to SEC and American accounting standards. But if they were listed on an American stock exchange, maybe they were. Regardless, I doubted it changed the gist of what he was telling me. "What would you do?"

"I assume these companies are really big, tens of billions in sales?"

I nodded. "Or more."

"And one billion is the actual total paid, not more?"

"Right again."

"Then I have two ideas. One, create a shell company, call it X, as a joint venture with each other, purportedly to develop some sort of technology that would appear to be useful to them. Capitalize X with the billion dollars. As a private company, X wouldn't be subject to public or regulatory scrutiny. X could use one of several methods to funnel the money to whomever. Then let X quietly fade away, just another failed tech joint venture."

I was scribbling furiously in my notebook.

"The second idea is a variation on the first. Instead of starting a new entity, invest in an existing private outfit that belongs to whomever you want to pay off. In this case, each company would invest separately, ostensibly for some technology mumbo-jumbo. Invest in the company, mind you, not buy the technology." He locked onto my eyes with his to stress the point.

"What's true in both cases is that an investment of that size, under a billion each, by a really big company is merely a footnote in its financial statement, and no one really pays much attention to how the investment pans out."

"Huh!"

Nick smiled broadly again. He was clearly enjoying himself.

"How could you discover this from the outside?"

"Well, they wouldn't announce it, so, from the outside, you'd need to know what you were looking for in a quarterly financial report. It would be a balance sheet item, not a P&L item. And it would be vague, like I said, either a footnote or a one-liner."

I wrote BALANCE SHEET and P&L in my notebook and underlined both twice; items to look up later. They don't teach this stuff in PI school.

"So, I couldn't just go to one of these companies and ask their CFO if they recently spent a few hundred million on something they didn't announce?"

"Not a chance. Look, the kind of companies you're talking about, they can easily pull this off without anyone being the wiser. I mean, no one is embezzling; probably the CEO and CFO, and maybe one or two other senior execs, have agreed they need to do this for the good of the business. The CEO gives some cock-and-bull story to the board and it's done with."

I'm sure he saw the disappointment on my face.

"If this wasn't just hypothetical, I'd be glad to look at the quarterly reports with you, see if we could spot something. Thing is, this quarter is about a month old, and last quarter's report is due soon. If this billion-dollar payment was made recently, you might have to wait three more months for a report. But no worry, right? It's just hypothetical?"

I calculated the likely dates. Nick was right, it would have been in the new quarter. *Shit!*

I had gotten what I came for, but, on a lark, I asked, "Did you know Rex Baker?"

"Rascal Rex? You bet."

"I never heard him called that."

"Yeah, well, he preferred the nickname he made up for himself, Mr. Perfect. Why do you ask about Rex Baker?"

I explained, superficially, my involvement with the case as investigator for the Public Defender. "The case is over, but I was sort of wondering about his partners at his old firm."

"Nolan DeWitt and Gavin Smart? What about them?"

"If you don't mind, just sort of tell me about them."

"DeWitt is an old-school VC. Now that he's in control of his own firm, he'll probably muddle along, but he doesn't really have what it takes in today's climate, and he's too full of himself to bring in younger, fresher talent."

"What about Gavin Smart?"

"I hear Gavin has retired. He's still young, but I say, good for him. You know, he and I used to boat together. We had adjacent slips at the same marina. That goes back ten, fifteen years."

"I got the impression he played second fiddle to DeWitt."

"Appearances can be deceptive. Gavin was twice the VC and businessman as Nolan DeWitt. Just not noisy about it."

It was mid-afternoon. I wanted to hear more from Nick Marchetti. I asked him if I could buy him dinner and pick his brain a bit more. He said I was in luck, his wife was spending a few days with his boss's wife, Lisa Gold, at her winery in Napa.

I have no idea what made me get on this track with Nick. I guess my subconscious mind was ahead of my conscious mind, and I was smart enough, or lucky enough, or most likely just impulsive enough, to go where it led.

* * *

After I left Nick Marchetti's office, I stopped by the hospital to see Boomer. Sally was with him, and they were happily chatting away. He said they had just negotiated with his doctor for what Boomer called "early release." He could go home with Sally tomorrow.

Had I heard right? Yes, I verified it. Boomer was going to stay at Sally's for a couple of days. I had never even been to Sally's place, and now she was taking in this old coot and nursing him!

Chapter 50

When I invited Nick Marchetti to dinner, I was immediately stuck as to where to go. Most of the places I knew were too noisy, crowded, or both for a private conversation in which you didn't have to shout to be heard or whisper not to be overheard. I was also worried about being able to afford the kind of upscale restaurant I figured Marchetti would be used to.

Nick had bailed me out by suggesting the nearby Paco's Picante Mexican restaurant, where the booths and tables gave privacy and the high ceilings deadened noise. It was also moderately priced.

After much discussion in Spanish and a trip to the kitchen by the waitress for a consultation, Nick somehow managed to order something off-menu called *picadillo*. At Nick's urging, I ordered it as well. The waitress brought it in a lidded pot that she put in the center of the table with a ladle so we could serve ourselves. She seemed especially pleased to serve it.

The dish involved ground beef, potatoes, onions and spices, and something I couldn't identify, which Nick revealed were raisins. It was delicious, and I said so.

Nick grinned with pleasure. "My old yacht captain used to make it for us. If a cook's Mexican, chances are they know how to make it."

It was, as they say, my peso, so I got right to it. "How did Rex Baker earn the nickname Rascal Rex?" I thought maybe Nick was anticipating this and was going to tell me it was because of Rex's sexual peccadillos while we enjoyed our *picadillo*. But it seemed that no such bilingual pun was intended.

"Rex often went against conventional wisdom. People would say, 'What's that rascal Rex up to now?' The nickname stuck."

"What sort of things did he do?"

"Well, most VCs believe in the land-grab theory. They push startups to grow the top line as quickly as possible and worry about profit later. Rex the contrarian would usually guide his entrepreneurs to position themselves for fat margins and let everyone else wear themselves out in the rush to the bottom. His approach took more patience, but it was hard to argue with the results."

Our waitress came by to see how we liked our dinner. We gave her two thumbs up and asked for another round of beverages.

"Here's another example," Nick said when she left. "You know what dark funds are?"

I was proud of myself. I had done my homework last night and knew what top line and margins meant. But not dark funds. I said so.

"Dark funds are investment funds that are kept sort of secret. They invest in startups that do classified work, dark projects for the government. DOD, CIA, NSA, like that. You don't get unicorns, but you can get decent research contracts to help fund startup costs, and if you're R&D is successful, fat margins over long term government contracts."

Notebook: unicorns, underlined twice. "Why are the funds secret?"

"Not so much secret as quiet. They tend to attract different investors than the usual VC funds. More patient and willing to settle for lower returns for less risk. The companies they fund tend to be secretive about their work, sometimes to an extreme."

Nick served up seconds for both of us.

"Why is there less risk?"

"That's where the VC really earns his keep. It's all about being sure the funding government agency is willing to pay enough, long enough, for the R&D. So even if it doesn't pan out, you don't lose money. It takes special skill to figure that out when you're dealing with contracts that no one admits exist and are buried so deep in the federal budget our elected officials can't find them."

"Rex was good at that?"

"No, that was Gavin. He had somehow gotten the right experience at an investment bank. Rex recruited Gavin just as he was starting Rex Baker Venture Partners in 2001. I remember that because it was right after the dot-com bubble burst. It was a tough time to be starting a VC firm. But Rascal Rex let Gavin have his head, and the timing was perfect. After September 11, there was an explosion of funding for dark projects. Dark funds carried Rex Baker Venture Partners through the early years."

Our waitress returned with our drinks.

"I'm curious. The Rex Baker case is solved, right? Your client is free?"

"The police have closed the case. David Novak is a free

man."

"So, you're just asking me about Rex because *you're* curious?"

"It's a hazard of my profession."

Nick grinned, but let it drop. We quietly enjoyed the rest of the *picadillo*.

As the table was cleared, I decided to take one more flyer with Nick. "Ever heard of Western Land Holdings?"

"Sure. Gavin's brainchild. Made him seriously rich."

* * *

According to Nick, Gavin Smart set up Western Land Holdings to buy and hold property until its price skyrocketed. Nick explained that land often appreciated in value in fits and starts. The value of a piece of property might stay in the doldrums for years, then take off, multiplying dramatically in value overnight because of the development going on or planned around it. Gavin's strategy was to buy seemingly useless property cheap and patiently wait for that development to occur.

In cities, he would buy a distressed lot and turn it into a parking lot. In the suburbs, he would build a mini-storage facility on cheap property; these, Nick said, were inexpensive to construct.

In either case, Western Land Holdings would lease the property on a year-to-year basis to someone to run their parking lot or self-storage business. The goal was to make enough from the lease to cover carrying costs, like loan payments, property tax and insurance. As the holdings grew in number, they provided collateral for loans used to buy more property. Thus, the Western Land Holdings portfolio grew to be worth hundreds of millions of dollars.

When the value of a piece of property suddenly took off, Western Land Holdings put the hapless tenant on notice that their lease would not be renewed and sold it, reaping huge gains that would be used for down payments for other property investments.

Nick started to explain about the tax angles of real estate investing, deferring capital gains and such, but I asked him to skip that. I was on information overload.

Bottom line was that Western Land Holdings had made its sole owner, Gavin Smart, a wealthy man, above and beyond what he made at Rex Baker Venture Partners. And I had a new candidate for Mastermind.

Chapter 51

My complementary DeepDig report on Odysseus Zorba arrived. It listed Zorba's occupation as research chemist, his employer from 2000 until 2007 as De Anza Research Laboratory in Palo Alto.

I could not find much about De Anza Research Laboratory online. I managed to piece together that it had been a private lab of some sort that, coincidentally, started in 2000 and folded in 2007. Its scientific director had been Dr. Odysseus Zorba. I found one other useful item, a one-liner in a listing of quarterly venture capital activity in 2002 that said De Anza Research Laboratory had secured funding from Rex Baker Venture Partners. Its industry category was listed as government research.

I searched around and found a list of the companies in each of the portfolios of the Rex Baker Venture Partners investment funds that were active in 2002. De Anza Research Laboratory was not included. Which would be the case if it had been in one of the secretive dark funds managed by Gavin Smart; those portfolios would not have been made public.

Since 2007, Zorba had been self-employed as a private consultant, a perfect way to hide your true employer. Other than his address at the Pescadero property, even DeepDig could provide few other details about him for the past decade. DeepDig did indicate that he'd had no activity on his credit report for several years. That was consistent with what folks in Pescadero had said, that he'd always paid cash when he came to town.

DeepDig had provided a lot of old information on Zorba, but almost nothing that was useful. While I was bemoaning this sorry situation, Sally and Boomer arrived for what she firmly insisted had to be a short meeting without coffee or donuts. "I have a class to teach. You two have two hours, then my patient is gone."

After Sally closed my office door behind her, Boomer said, "I haven't been mothered like this since I was a tyke." He had a twinkle in his eyes. *What,* I wondered, *have you done with the real Sally Rocket? Would this imposter Sally soon start posting on Pinterest?*

I filled Boomer in on my conversations with Nick Marchetti. My excitement at the emergence of Gavin Smart as my Mastermind prime suspect overwhelmed my disappointment at the DeepDig on Zorba. Boomer agreed that Smart looked like a good candidate, but his enthusiasm was a lot more subdued than mine.

"I hate to be a spoil-sport," he said, "but what do we actually have? Zorba's old company was funded by an investment fund Smart managed, and Smart's company owns the property Zorba's occupied for ten years. Not exactly a smoking gun."

Or a smoking ShushNik. "You're right."

"Remember that Novak's old company was funded by Rex Baker? Didn't make him guilty. And you were all hot and bothered by Storm Crusher. Smart knew Zorba way back when, and had a property available when Zorba's outfit went tits-up. So what?"

I raised my hands to ward off the verbal blows. "Okay," I said glumly, "we don't have enough."

"Not hardly. We have no evidence linking the exploding ShushNik to Zorba. Even if we did, we have no hard evidence linking Smart to working with or funding Zorba. And anyone could be at the other end of the money trail for Tahara and Ambrose."

The wind was definitely out of my sails. "I thought Sally had you all cheerful." I think the way I said it, Boomer got the subtext.

"Look, young fella, I may be a randy old goat, but Sally's just a real good friend. She says I remind her of her grandpa, just several shades lighter."

Duly admonished, I got a soda from the fridge. Boomer, following Sally's orders, took a bottle of water.

"I know it's him," I said.

"Probably is."

As with Storm Crusher, I thought a rich guy like Smart would be too well insulated and protected for us to investigate directly. It had been different with Rex Baker and family. Not only was Rex dead, but I'd had the power of the Public Defender's office behind me. Now, I had no standing whatsoever.

Boomer was right. For all the investigating, we still didn't have much. Just before Sally came to collect him, he asked a question I hadn't given much thought.

"Suppose we do build a good case. What do we do with it?"

"Turn it over to the cops, I guess."

Boomer squinted at me. "Yeah, but which cops?"

Damn good question.

* * *

Detective Rice called to let me know that he was going public through the press in an attempt to identify Mute Man. He used the courtesy call as an opportunity to goose me for any sort of lead as to who the guy might be or why he might have accosted me. I still had nothing for him.

Less than 20 minutes later, Sylvia Sanchez called. "I've got a client who seems to have found his way into your office, uninvited."

"Hello to you, too," I said.

Ignoring the snark, she plowed ahead. "Through some misunderstanding, you felt threatened and summoned help. Then your civilian girlfriend subdued my client. With, I might add, excessive force."

"You forgot to mention his gun."

"Part of the misunderstanding."

"Are you getting all defense attorney on me?"

"Sorry, Joe, force of habit. I am unofficially, off the record, asking you to help us identify this jackass who refuses to communicate and assist in his own defense."

"An odd thing to ask the victim. Did Rice put you up to this?"

"I just got off the phone with the good detective."

"I promise to do everything I can to help identify my assailant."

When it became clear that I didn't mean I had anything more for her at this time, Sylvia thanked me and ended the call.

Good citizen that I am, I decided to help as promised. Okay, that wasn't my motivation. With everything that was going on, I had neglected pursuing Mute Man's link to Mastermind, which now meant his connection to Gavin Smart. Had I waited just a bit longer before I hit the panic button, he might have said something useful. In fact, the more I thought about it, the more certain I was he was about to do that when I sounded the alarm.

I had instantly panicked. Sally had told me to forget it, that was what a panic button was for. But I had let Spenser and Elvis down. I was a PI, I had to show more courage. I vowed to do better in the future.

Of course, I could have ended up dead doing that. Ah, the risks we PIs take in the pursuit of justice!

I dug around and found the photos I had taken of Mute Man that evening as he lay on the floor of my office. I had an excellent closeup of his face. He had the kind of plain vanilla face you look right past, one you instantly forget. I posted the shot on social media, asking the Internet for help identifying him.

I didn't know it at the time, but Mute Man was now doomed.

* * *

"Ain't that your boy?"

The elderly woman, sitting on a rocking chair on the front porch of her assisted living facility, took her glasses hanging around her neck and, with arthritic fingers, slowly put them on. She squinted at the picture her friend was pointing at on her iPad.

"Sure looks like him. What's it say?"

"Says he's in jail. Says he won't talk to anyone."

"Gotta go help my boy," the old woman said.

Chapter 52

"How did you know?" Ryan Baker sounded surprised when he took my call.

"Know what?"

"Mother is missing again."

I had called to see if I could get any useful information about Gavin Smart from Ryan or his mother. I had no idea what he was talking about.

"Missing?"

"She's been gone for three days. Just took off. No note, no word from her, nothing."

"Maybe I can help."

"Why the hell not? Come on over."

* * *

The gate to the Baker estate swung open after I showed my face to a machine next to the abandoned guard shack and gave my name to a disembodied female voice. I drove along the long driveway, parked, and was greeted at the massive front door by a maid. She escorted me to the patio by the pool, where I had interviewed Ryan and Danica Baker when I first started on this case. That was just a couple of months ago, though it seemed like much longer.

Ryan stood and greeted me. We shook hands and sat. I mentioned the lack of security personnel.

"Oh, yeah. I guess the last time you were here was right after Rex died, and we had guards to keep news crews and gawkers under control. That was unusual. My father didn't like personal security people hanging around, and we rarely used them. Still don't."

"So, about your mother."

"I had no idea this was coming. I should have recognized the early signs of a manic episode. Hell, I've seen enough of them. But she's been doing so well. I swear, there were no signs at all. She was stable on her meds, seeing her psychiatrist regularly. She was so...normal."

I had to get him to stop the *mea culpa* and focus on specifics. "What exactly happened?"

"She went on an outing to Stanford Shopping Center with Edita."

"Edita?"

"Edita Horvath, one of her aides. Except at night, Mom's always got an aide around. At night, the house is alarmed in case she tries to sneak out. Anyway, it was a routine shopping trip, completely ordinary. Mom was trying on clothes at one of the boutiques. Edita waited for her outside the dressing room area. Mom was in there a long time, Edita became concerned and went to check on her. Mom was gone. Turns out there was an exterior door, through a storage room, behind the dressing rooms. She must have gone out that way."

"She'd been to that shop before?"

"It was one of her favorites."

"Who's looking for her?" If I was to help, I had to figure

out how to work with whoever Ryan had already engaged, to avoid a turf battle.

Ryan scrunched his brow. He seemed puzzled by the question. "I went through the usual drill and filed a missing person report."

The local cops would be on the lookout and maybe inform other jurisdictions, but no one would be actively looking for Danica Baker. She wasn't a little girl or someone's sweet old grandma. I kept that disheartening piece of information to myself, but my face must have given something away, because Ryan got all defensive.

"Look, she always calls after a few days, asking to be picked up from wherever. The thing is, Dad always handled this stuff. This is the first time it's happened since..."

"Tell me. Ryan, what do you do if you have a toothache?"

He gave me an odd look. "Go to the dentist? Oh, I get it. You think I need a private investigator. You may be right. Dad was probably too cavalier."

I got interested in my lemonade as I waited for Ryan to connect the dots. I could almost see the lightbulb click on over his head.

"Uh, Joe, are you available? I'll gladly pay your usual rate."

Actually, Ryan Baker would be paying my new clueless-rich-client rate. Plus expenses.

My motives were impure. I wanted this case because I badly needed the money. I was being opportunistic and elbowing my way into being hired.

At no time did it occur to me that this was anything more sinister than another in Danica Baker's long history of manic episodes. Just like it had not occurred to me at first that Mute Man may have been sent my way by Mastermind after Boomer and I went sniffing around Pescadero asking about Zorba.

I needed to become more skeptical about coincidences. Or at least somewhat skeptical.

Chapter 53

I told myself that I needed to focus on Danica Baker's disappearance while the trail was still hot, that she might be in danger and need me to rescue her. My damsel in distress hero complex was going full tilt.

The truth was that probably 90% of my motivation for jumping in whole hog was that I was so frustrated by feeling stalled in what I now thought of as the Mastermind case, I wanted to lose myself in something else, and finding Danica would likely be a textbook exercise in Private Investigation 101. I even had a missing-person checklist from a PI course I had taken. I was looking forward to having the satisfaction of properly conducting and closing a case. I got right on it.

Ryan swore that he and his mother were getting along well. No arguments or other problems. "We always get along just fine." He had nothing useful for me.

I interviewed Edita Horvath, who confirmed what Ryan Baker had told me. She also said that she usually took Mrs. Baker shopping because she covered the day shift. Edita checked her calendar; they had last been to that boutique a month ago.

Danica carried her driver's license but her son kept her passport in his safe. She had a single credit card with a very low credit limit. She had an ATM card with access to a checking account in which Ryan kept about $1,000, strictly for access to cash. Edita and Ryan figured she'd probably had a few hundred dollars with her. Danica didn't have a lot of resources, but still enough to travel pretty much anywhere in the country.

With Ryan's help getting access, I reviewed Danica's checking account and credit card transactions. There had been no unusual activity leading up to the vanishing act and no activity since she disappeared.

Danica's cell phone had been found in the boutique's dressing room. Ryan knew the password and she hadn't changed it. Together, we looked at her recent calls and text messages. Ryan confirmed that they were to and from the usual suspects, their content was unremarkable, and none were recent. Her Facebook activity was boring.

I searched Danica's room. The maid had kept it neat and tidy, but she said that was how Danica had left it. According to Ryan and Edita, nothing seemed to be missing that Danica wouldn't have routinely been wearing or carrying in her handbag, with one exception. It appeared that Danica had taken all her medication with her. I found no hidden letters, notes or photos. Her laptop computer seemed to be used only for web browsing. Her search history made me yawn.

Ryan reinforced the clueless label I had bestowed on him when he admitted that he had no information about his mother's previous disappearing acts, just the vague memories of a kid. Perhaps I was being unfair; he *had* been a kid. His father had handled everything. All he knew was that she had always gone to Las Vegas. He had no idea where she had stayed. He didn't even know how she used to get there, whether she had flown, taken a bus, or whatever.

The clueless son who had been just sitting around waiting for something to happen now seemed energized by my activity. He suggested we head to Vegas and show Danica's picture around. I pointed out that there were an awful lot of hotels and motels in Sin City, let alone nearby towns. I looked it up. There were over 30 hotels on the Strip alone, over 100,000 rooms. Talk about looking for a needle in a haystack.

I needed to give Ryan something to do. I convinced him to swallow his pride and set him to work calling friends, in the off chance they had any idea where his mother was or she had said something that might help us locate her.

I called the police station and got someone in missing persons to look up whatever they had on Danica Baker's prior disappearances. She found the reports in the files. In each case, Rex had merely called to say his wife was home, safe and sound. There were no details noted, just another check box on a closed missing person report. She commented that this was the typical disposition of these cases.

I interviewed the rest of the staff, including Manuela, the aide who came on duty late afternoon. Ryan still had Edita and her coming to work every day. They had seen nothing unusual in Danica's behavior.

By the time I left the Baker estate for the day, I had filled my notebook and gone through much of my checklist, but still had no clues as to Danica's whereabouts. But I had an impression, one I decided to keep to myself for the time being.

* * *

Getting into jail was easy. Act drunk, sprawl out on the sidewalk in Santana Row in the evening, annoy the restaurant-goers, argue loudly and threateningly with the two cops who try to roust you, and poof, you gain admittance with a 30-day reservation and free room and board.

Once inside, getting a shiv was also easy. Make a contact inside, tell your pre-arranged visitor to give $100 to the contact's friend outside, and poof, you're armed.

Using the shiv was easiest of all. The mute dude had no friends, no circle of protection. It was a cinch to stick him in the crowded exercise yard, then melt away into the throng of noisy, but never nosey, prisoners. Dargo bled out before guards could get him medical attention.

Easiest ten grand he'd ever made.

Chapter 54

Danica Baker's psychiatrist was willing to give me a few minutes before his first appointment. That meant I had to get up at what, to me, was the crack of dawn, and battle rush-hour traffic across the valley to get to his Palo Alto office at 8:30 a.m. We sat in Dr. Kim's cramped office. It was obviously not his consulting room, it was all business.

"Some ground rules first, Mr. Brink. Patient confidentiality. Because Mr. Baker is her conservator, I can disclose information to him, but that does not carry over to a third party."

Ryan had already spoken with Dr. Kim, who had told him that he had seen no signs of Danica entering a manic episode. He also said she had, in his opinion, been doing very well and seemed stable on her meds.

"I understand," I said. "I'm really here to learn a little more about bipolar disorder in general. Like, what leads to these disappearing episodes."

"It's a combination of stress and the underlying illness. A person with bipolar disorder has the potential to have a manic episode. We can control that with medication, but not eliminate it. If that manic potential leaks out, you get an episode. Sometimes, it leaks out on its own. Other times, stress plus potential equals an episode."

"So, it can happen with no stress, but the more stress, the more likely?"

Dr. Kim smiled. "That sums it up nicely."

"Why do they run off?"

"Not all do. Mania is accompanied by feeling of grandiosity, increased energy, and disinhibition. They feel larger than life. In the extreme, the patient has delusions. Put that all together, and they often take off for excitement and adventure."

"Ryan told me her last episode was just before her husband died. Did you see that one coming?"

Dr. Kim became thoughtful. "I want to help you without breaking confidentiality. Mrs. Baker has been doing quite well for some time now. That predates her last hospitalization. In the past, I sensed when she was having difficulty, though that did not always mean she would have an episode. That last time, I was taken by surprise."

"Just like this time?"

"Just like this time," he said.

* * *

The manager of the very upscale clothing boutique greeted me with a nervous smile and a tentative handshake. As with Dr. Kim, I had Ryan set up our meeting.

"My name is Ashley Carter. I'm pleased to meet you, Mr. Brink."

Her worried expression and tired eyes belied her words. She looked like a weary former fashion model, tall and skinny, with perfect hair and makeup, and a smart looking outfit that fit her perfectly. Her name sounded like the brand name for a line of women's clothing or a chain of shops just like the one we were in. I kept that thought to myself.

"Mrs. Baker is a very good customer, with excellent taste."

Meaning she came in often and spent a lot. I wondered if she ever said such a customer had lousy taste.

"Were you here when she went out the back?"

Her hands fluttered like birds. "Yes, I was. But I was not waiting on Mrs. Baker."

I didn't need her to get defensive. "I want to assure you that no one thinks you or your staff did anything wrong. I just need some help figuring out where she might have gone. And that seems to start here. Can you show me the dressing room?"

It was still early, and the rooms were not in use. We walked through that area to a door in the back that had a small "employees only" sign.

"I guess she went out this way."

The door opened into a large room where clothing and accessories were stored. We walked past the stock to double back doors that opened to the outside walkway. She used a key to open it. Once outside, Ashley gestured off in the distance. "Delivery trucks park in the parking lot. They cart the merchandise here."

"This door is locked from the outside?"

"Always."

"What about from the inside."

She shaded her eyes from the sun. "I'm afraid we used to keep it unlocked except when we locked up at night."

"So, anyone could have walked through the dressing area and out the way we just did," I said.

"Then, yes. But not anymore. The back door is now locked except when we're receiving deliveries."

Something about locking the barn door came to mind. I let it pass. "This door isn't alarmed?"

"Just when we're closed."

I noticed a security camera over the back door. Ryan had already arranged for me to view the store's security footage for the time in question. As we went back inside, I asked Ashley Carter about that.

"I don't have access to it, but our IT guy is supposed to be here at one o'clock to help you."

It was lunch time. I headed across the mall to Max's for a deli sandwich.

* * *

The IT guy was punctual and cooperative. There were no security cameras in the dressing area, but there were two in the stock room. The day she took off, Danica walked through the stock room and out the back door. She wore a hat with a big floppy brim and a black blouse with black slacks. The hat and blouse were items she had brought into the dressing room ostensibly to try on. She had left the bright red blouse she came in with behind. They had also found the tags she had removed from the hat and blouse.

It wasn't a great disguise, but good enough to give her some extra time to make her escape.

I also looked at footage for the last time she had been in the shop, which we deduced from Edita's log and her credit card charges. There was Danica, entering the stock room from the interior door and opening, then immediately shutting, the exterior door. Planning her future route.

With the cooperation of mall security, again arranged by Ryan, I was able to track her route on the day she split, from camera to camera, out to the parking lot. Along the way, she used her phone, apparently to send a text message. But she had left her cell phone in the shop. So, she had a second phone.

By the time Danica Baker reached the parking lot, a Lincoln Town Car was waiting for her at the curb. I knew it was waiting for her because the video showed the driver standing by the rear door, then opening it for her right away.

The security video was too grainy to provide anything to help identify the Town Car. This wasn't TV, where they could always magically zoom in and enhance the image and pull up the license plate.

My last view of Danica Baker was of her whipping off her hat and gracefully entering the back seat.

* * *

"You're saying she planned this with someone else?" Ryan seemed incredulous as we again sat by the pool.

"She cased the boutique well in advance. She had a second phone that no one here knew about. She was picked up almost instantly by a private car."

Ryan shook his head in bewilderment.

"I bet she never took her meds with her when she took off in the past," I said.

"I really don't know, but you're probably right. You think maybe this wasn't a manic thing?"

"Maybe. The question is, who was her accomplice?"

"I have no idea. That's why I hired you."

He was right. I also had come to the end of my checklist. *Okay, Mr. Detective, time to detect.*

"One thing you could help me with, just so I have a complete picture. When did you learn that Rex was terminal?"

Ryan thought a moment. "It was about a month before he was killed."

"Did your mother know?"

"Yeah, he told us together. Why do you ask?"

"No particular reason. Like I said, it was a loose end. Sometimes my job is just collecting miscellaneous pieces of information. Most of it doesn't turn out to mean anything to the case, but you can never tell ahead of time which will be important."

As I headed home, I experienced the joy of Silicon Valley's late-afternoon rush hour. *How do people do this every day?* As I merged from 280 onto 85, the traffic went from a crawl to a dead stop.

Which was where I was on both of my big cases.

Chapter 55

The morning paper featured a big story about O.J. Simpson, the football star who had been acquitted for murdering his ex-wife and her boyfriend in 1994. The news was that Simpson was being released from prison after serving nine years for an unrelated armed robbery.

I knew the O.J. murder case had been big news in the '90s, but I was just a kid at the time and didn't know much about it. Now I read the story with interest, including all the background stuff which I was unfamiliar with. It was a heck of a story and a good distraction from my detecting frustrations.

The front page of the local section interested me even more. The lead headline was "Silent Prisoner Slain." Once again, the story had missed the deadline for the newspaper yesterday, so it was today that I read about it. I guess letting me know my assailant had been killed was not on either Sylvia's or Detective Rice's to-do list.

The county jail was a rough place, but it was not often that a prisoner was murdered. The death of an inmate was an embarrassment to the Sheriff's Department and our very political sheriff. It had not helped that this came just days after the police asked for help identifying the silent victim, who apparently had not even uttered a sound when he'd been stabbed to death. The sheriff was quoted as saying that they would get to the bottom of this, that such violence in her jail would not be tolerated, yada, yada, yada.

I called Boomer. Sally had reluctantly taken him home yesterday. He said he was doing as well as an old coot could hope for.

Boomer hadn't heard about Mute Man, and neither of us knew what to make of his murder. "If we're right that he was sent after you by Mastermind," Boomer said, "and if he kept quiet out of loyalty or fear, it could be Mastermind who ordered the jail hit to be sure he stayed quiet."

"That would certainly have been misplaced loyalty," I said.

"But not misplaced fear," Boomer said.

Unsaid was that if we were also right that Gavin Smart was Mastermind, he had not only fooled me completely when we had met, he was one cold-hearted bastard.

* * *

Mr. Vu came into my office. It was unusually early in the day for me to see him; his office hours seemed to be mainly in the evening.

"Good news! I have just been appointed Mr. Chu's conservator. Mr. Chu is now in the same nursing home as your grandfather. He seems content and told me he feels safe there. Thank you so much for that referral and all of your help."

I was happy for Vu and Chu. At least one case had gone well.

I also got a call from David Novak. Storm Crusher was

investing in ShushTek, and they were going after deals to license ShushNik technology to cellphone manufacturers and anyone else who would pay them royalties. The subtext of our conversation was that David was looking to the future and ready to put the whole sorry *VC Pie* affair behind him. I was happy for him, too.

The short story was that David Novak had gone on *VC Pie* and ended up landing Storm Crusher as an investor. Boring. But then there was the long story...

* * *

Ryan Baker didn't bother to say hello. "You can stop looking for my mother. I know where she is. Well, not exactly where, but I know who she's with and that she's okay."

"Tell me," I said.

"My lawyer just called. He just received a copy of a petition that was filed in court to substitute Gavin Smart for me as Mom's conservator. He says it's obvious that Mom is with Smart, wherever he is. I have a meeting with him later today to get the details."

"Can I join you?"

"Why not?"

I should have been stunned. Instead, I felt an odd sense of calm. Everything I had stumbled over associated with Rex Baker's murder was part of one big puzzle, and the pieces were about to be rearranged yet again.

This was my first big, juicy, complex case, the kind I had yearned for when I decided to become an independent private investigator. I needed to get used to how these things unfolded, to the unexpected twists and turns.

I also wondered at the coincidence of having two unrelated issues dealing with conservatorship come up during the same morning. That was something else I had to get used to. Sometimes a coincidence was just two similar things accidentally happening at about the same.

The thing I had to learn was how to recognize when it was no accident.

Chapter 56

Ryan Baker must generate a lot of billings for Fortunato, Hennings and Kuperman, because Scott Fortunato left his office palace and came to the Baker estate for our meeting, scheduled on short notice. Ryan had told me that Fortunato had been the family's lawyer for as long as he could remember. Of course, he was probably charging Ryan some preposterous hourly rate that included travel time and every minute he thought about the Bakers while sitting in the john.

My drive across the valley mid-afternoon and opposite commuter traffic took about a third as long as yesterday. Still, it had given me time to think about this development. I was forming a hypothesis, and would now see how it held up to the facts. I was feeling a bit full of myself, calling it a hypothesis, but I figured at the hourly rate Ryan was paying me, I needed to up my vocabulary.

The poolside was clearly where Ryan conducted most business. Fortunato was already chatting with him, though I was spot on time. Scott Fortunato was casting-call perfect for the part of the mature, powerful lawyer to the rich and famous. Sixtyish, a bit over six feet tall, trim, with a good tan, freshly barbered silver hair, and icy blue eyes. His suit cost more than my monthly rent. Heck, his tie probably cost more than my car payment. When Fortunato spoke, he exuded gravitas.

We shook hands. His grip was firm. “I’m please to meet you, Mr. Brink. Ryan has explained your role here.” His expression said he did not completely approve of my presence, but was humoring his client.

“Please, call me Joe.”

He did not ask me to call him Scott. I gathered that privilege was reserved for Ryan, the man paying the bill.

We sat around the circular table with a sweating pitcher of lemonade. A multi-page document lay on the table, squarely before the lawyer. I detected that it was the court filing.

“Scott was just telling me that this is a very clever legal move,” Ryan said

“How so?”

Fortunato answered, but he addressed Ryan, not me.

“First, let me clarify something. I’m not the family lawyer in this situation. I’m your attorney, Ryan. Your mother has acquired other legal representation and that’s who filed this action.”

“Okay.”

“Now, they aren’t contesting the conservatorship. They assert simply that Mrs. Baker wishes to change the conservator.”

“Why is that clever?” I persisted.

Still making eye-contact with Ryan, Fortunato said, “If they contested the conservatorship, we could bring in her entire psychiatric history. Instead, the only question is whether or not she is of sound enough mind to understand the consequences of getting a different conservator. That’s not a very high standard of mental health, nor are those consequences particularly onerous. They've even attached a report from a psychiatrist who has just examined your mother and asserts that she is competent to make this decision."

"Doesn't this assume Gavin Smart is an appropriate conservator?" I said.

Still to Ryan, "I'm afraid that's also not a high standard. Pretty much any responsible adult can serve, and the court favors someone acceptable to the conservatee."

Ryan appeared bewildered by this entire discussion. "Doesn't she at least have to give me a reason for wanting the change?"

Fortunato gestured to the papers in front of him. "It says she feels imprisoned, that being watched all the time by aides you employ is onerous. She's wanting a more normal life."

Ryan looked stricken. "But the aides were something my father originally set up, and it was for her own good. Mom had final say in who we hired and never once complained. I mean, she sometimes complained about a specific aide, and then we replaced them. But she never griped about having them."

"That may be true, but it's still extraordinary for a mental health conservatorship. I doubt the judge will have seen many other situations where a conservatee who was not institutionalized or didn't have complex physical problems had fulltime aides. Maybe none. Few people could or would afford it, let alone like it."

Ryan appeared astonished at this. Born with a silver spoon in his mouth, surrounded by servants, he had trouble grasping how the other 99.9% lived. This wasn't exactly

Downton Abbey, but is was far from normal living.

"I don't understand any of this," Ryan said, clenching his fists, his voice rising. "If she was so unhappy, she should have just told me."

"You had no indications?" Fortunato said. He sounded skeptical.

Ryan slowly shook his head. "I've racked my brain. I'm telling you, there wasn't the slightest clue. I thought we were close. We got along fine, everything was normal." It was Ryan's turn to point to the papers. "Then this."

"No disagreements? No arguments?"

"Mom came and went pretty much as she wanted. One of the aides would drive her, sure, but they knew how to be unobtrusive when she was with friends or something."

Fortunato persisted. "No money problems?"

"She has plenty, you know that. She had access to her money, but she had to go through me for anything major. Still, I don't ever recall saying no."

Fortunato drummed his fingers on the glass tabletop. I wanted to ask Ryan how he would feel living in his mom's situation, with a constant babysitter and needing to ask her son for her allowance. I stifled the urge.

After a few moments of silence, Ryan asked, "Can't I challenge this?"

"You can, Ryan, but unless she has a complete psychotic episode in the courtroom, or we can prove that Mr. Smart is unfit to serve or has coerced your mother, we will surely lose."

"I think I can help you there, Mr. Fortunato," I said.

For the first time since we sat down, Scott Fortunato

turned to face me. He cocked his head and raised his eyebrows, as if just realizing I was still there.

I gave a succinct summary of the Mastermind case theory that Boomer and I had settled on. I left out all the extraneous details, blind alleys, and wrong assumptions I had made to get to this point. Throughout, Ryan looked dumfounded; Fortunato appeared fascinated.

When I was finished, a hush descended, as when the Pope raises his hands in St. Peter's Square. I was suddenly aware of the sound of birds chirping. After this went on a few moments, I pushed back my chair. "I could use a bathroom break."

"I think we could all use a little break, Joe. And by the way, call me Scott."

Chapter 57

Five minutes later, I was the first back to the pool patio. Ryan reappeared from the west wing of the house about 20 minutes later. His eyes were red, and he looked like he had taken a shower. His hair was damp and he had exchanged his T-shirt and shorts for a golf shirt and jeans.

After another 10 minutes, Scott came out of the main wing. "Sorry for the delay. I needed to cancel some appointments. I expect we're in for a long discussion."

"Can you both stay for dinner?" Ryan said.

"I can stay as long as needed," Scott said.

Ka-ching, I thought. I said, "Me, too." I also had a meter running. I could learn a thing or two from this guy Scott.

Ryan took out his phone and tapped it a couple of times. Almost instantly, a young woman came onto the patio from the east wing and walked to Ryan's side.

"We're going to have dinner out here," Ryan said. "What would you gentlemen like?"

He said that as if we could order anything and his kitchen would produce it. More, he said it as if that were of course the case. In my house, you looked in the fridge first to see what you could have.

Tonight, the kitchen would not be challenged. When I asked for a chicken Caesar salad, the others decided it was a terrific idea.

Once the young lady was out of earshot, Scott took charge. "Ryan, you are the client. We work for you. So, I need to ask you, first, what's your priority? To retain conservatorship or bring your father's killer to justice?"

"Can't we do both?"

"Of course we'll try, but just for the sake of argument, assume we can only do one. What then?"

"In that case, I'd just want what's best for my mom, But I don't really care about the conservatorship itself."

Scott nodded sagely. "It's just a means to an end."

"Yes, that's it."

"Okay, good," Scott said. "Now I want to address the elephant in the room. I'm sorry Ryan, but we absolutely must discuss this. Is it possible that your mother had something to do with Rex's death?"

Ryan looked at me. "Is that why you asked me when exactly we found out that Rex was terminal?"

"Yes."

"So," Scott said, "just theoretically, she could have been involved in the plot before she knew he was dying?"

"I don't want to even think about that," Ryan said. "But, yeah, she could have."

"Do we want to know?" I said.

Scott looked at me and smiled. "Excellent point. You know, I don't do criminal law, but my colleagues who do rarely want to know if their client is guilty."

"That's what I was thinking about," I said.

Ryan looked from me to Scott and back like he was watching a tennis match. "I don't follow you."

Scott explained about a criminal defense attorney needing to defend a client vigorously regardless of guilt or innocence. He also touched on the suborning perjury issue.

Looking confused, Ryan said, “I still don’t see what that’s got to do with any of this.”

“Joe is suggesting we assume your mother had nothing to do with the murder plot, and proceed on that basis,” Scott said.

“Okay,” Ryan said, “it *is* what I assume.”

“Then I won’t even look for any involvement on her part,” I said. I had picked up on the we part of the “we work for you” thing Scott had said, but I still wanted to make it clear I was on the case and part of Scott’s team.

There was another elephant in the room, or, I thought, more like a whale by the pool. Time to get at it. “Why would your mother turn to Gavin Smart?”

“The guy you think killed my father? I’m sorry, I can’t wrap my head around this.”

Scott reached out and put his hand on Ryan’s shoulder. It almost looked affectionate. “Just focus on Joe’s question, Ryan. Why Gavin?”

Ryan slowly shook his head and took a deep breath. “Gavin’s been a friend of the family for a long time. He was over here a lot when Dad was alive, and since then he’s been a comfort to Mom.”

So much for Gavin’s claim that he didn’t know the family very well, that Rex kept his private life separate from business.

“I get it,” Ryan said. “You think they’re having an affair?”

“What do you think?” Scott said.

Ryan shrugged, then shook his head. "I think it's possible," he said bleakly.

"It would explain this clever legal maneuver," Scott said. "The question is, how long have they been involved?"

"It could be for quite a while," Ryan said. "Do we need to get into this?"

"For the case? Maybe not," Scott said. "Let's just put it aside for now."

A relationship gave Danica and Gavin motive in Rex's murder. Individually or together. Especially if the plot started before Danica knew Rex was dying. But I decided to keep that to myself for now. Ryan didn't need me to add to his emotional load.

We were interrupted by the arrival of dinner and a brief wine discussion that ensued. We all agreed we could use some. I left the selection to Ryan and Scott. As long as it was white and cold, I'd be happy.

By unspoken agreement, we didn't talk about the case while we ate. Scott asked if any of us had seen the week-long series on Venezuela's political, social and economic collapse in the *Mercury News*. He said his wife was Venezuelan and her family members there were struggling with the meltdown.

After a decade of strongman Hugo Chávez's disastrous socialist regime, followed by several years of increasing chaos under his equally despotic successor, Nicolás Maduro, Venezuela was falling apart. Inflation was preposterous. Even basic necessities like food and medical supplies were scarce. There were daily protests, riots in the streets, brutal repression rampant and lawlessness. As the nation was descending into anarchy, many Chávez-Maduro cronies had been busy looting the country, sending its wealth overseas, and fleeing themselves. The big news was that a ring that smuggled these crooks and their ill-gotten gains into Northern California had been broken up by the FBI and ICE, and more arrests and deportations were expected.

I had read the newspaper reports; Ryan had not. Scott said that he had offered to help get his wife's relatives out of the country, but they chose to stay. For them, he said, home was home.

After our plates were cleared, we finished the last of the delicious wine, decided against having desert, and took another bathroom break.

* * *

"The question is," Scott said when we resumed, "how do we get Smart's link to Rex's murder into the conservatorship hearing? The other side will surely say that the police have closed the Rex Baker murder case, and our fantastic theory is little more than an irrelevant fantasy. The judge will almost certainly agree. We need to persuade him otherwise. I'll get some of my associates working on that first thing in the morning."

"I was thinking about the O.J. Simpson case," I said.

Poor Ryan looked more bewildered than ever. Scott, on the other hand, looked delighted.

"You are one clever fellow, Joe Brink."

Ryan was even younger than me. He was clueless as to who O.J. Simpson was, let alone his murder case.

Scott explained that in 1995, ex-NFL and movie star O.J.

Simpson had been acquitted for murdering his ex-wife, Nicole Brown Simpson, and her friend Ron Goldman in a circus of a trial in L.A. The Goldman family then filed and won a wrongful death suit.

"Here's the part that's important for us," Scott explained. "The standard of proof in criminal court, where Simpson was acquitted, is 'beyond a reasonable doubt.' But the standard in a civil case is 'preponderance of evidence.' It's a much lower standard, easier to win a judgement."

Ryan again looked confused. "So, he was tried twice for the same thing? I thought you couldn't do that."

"The first trial was a criminal trial where he faced prison, maybe even the death penalty. The civil case was a survivors' lawsuit for monetary damages. It was an uncommon legal maneuver. The Goldman's were awarded a judgement for something like $30 million."

"What's that do for us? I'm not interested in his money."

"Assume, for all the reasons Joe told us, the authorities won't reopen your father's murder case, won't investigate Gavin Smart. You can file a civil suit against him instead."

"What does that have to do with the conservatorship?"

"We file before the conservatorship hearing. It gets the whole story of the plot leading up to your father's death out there," Scott said. "He'll probably drop the conservatorship petition, or your mother will back out. At the very least, it will help make our case that he's not fit to serve. More, we could actually win a civil judgement based on mostly circumstantial evidence that would never get us a criminal conviction."

"Here's the thing, Ryan," I said. "Gavin has no idea that I or anyone else has connected him to the *VC Pie* plot. He has no idea you know he had Rex murdered. He has no idea the can of worms he's opened."

Ryan brightened for the first time since I'd seen him that day. "Let's go get the motherfucker."

I don't think the pun was intentional.

Chapter 58

Money is a wonderful thing. As in having lots of it.

In the three days since we had met at the Baker estate, Scott Fortunato had gotten DeepDig reports on everyone associated with the case. That included Gavin Smart, Nolan DeWitt, Hudson Ambrose, Becky and Lindsey Tahara, David and Anna Novak; the list went on and on. He even got reports on Danica and Ryan Baker as well as Boomer and me.

“Better to have information and not need it than need it and not have it,” was how Scott explained this to Ryan and me at the now familiar poolside table.

He had also, as he put it, “approached law enforcement and national security agencies at various levels.” He was uniformly told that they had no further interest in either the Rex Baker murder case or the explosive device that had killed him. Don’t bother us, we have far more important matters to attend to.

“We filed notice opposing the change in conservator. We also formally asked the state and local police to find Danica Baker and return her here, because you, Ryan, are concerned about your mentally ill mother’s well-being and, as her conservator, have the right and responsibility to determine where she lives and assure she has proper care. I don’t expect them to move aggressively on that, at least not yet. But we've gone on record."

Scott made a show of looking at his watch. Even I, whose only timepiece was my cellphone, recognized that it cost a fortune. "In less than an hour, the legal shit will hit the fan. We are filing a $100 million wrongful death suit against Gavin Smart."

The suit, Scott said, named Smart as mastermind of a plot to kill Rex Baker and take his mentally ill wife and her money for his own. He enlisted Becky Tahar, Hudson Ambrose, Odysseus Zorba and a John Doe—the Silent Prisoner—to carry out his scheme. To cover his tracks, he had those four murdered as well.

Scott acknowledged that he had picked up the word mastermind from me. "We lawyers are trained to shamelessly appropriate the good ideas of others. We are the masters of cut-and-paste. We call it precedent and research."

The only thing left out of the suit was the auction for the PAD technology. Scott said we didn't need it, and it was so over-the-top that it could bring the entire narrative into question. He also said that his inquiries at the federal level brought veiled but firm suggestions we should avoid the matter entirely.

* * *

News of the civil suit naming Gavin Smart as the mastermind behind the Perfect Murder fairly exploded on every form of news media. It had everything: sex, violence, money, intrigue, technology, even a murdered, mute John Doe. It was so juicy, you could almost see the news readers and commentators salivating.

This morning was the first court appearance. Scott was holding a carefully planned and staged impromptu press conference on the courthouse steps, before a mob of reporters and cameras, backed by an even larger crowd of looky-loos. Ryan stood somberly at his side. I had taken a position up a few steps, out of camera range, the action to my left.

Scott was careful to stick to the script. For each question, he replied with a nearly verbatim quote from the lawsuit, even if it meant not exactly answering the question. He carefully positioned Danica Baker as the mentally ill victim of the evil Gavin Smart. He adroitly managed to compare him to both Svengali and Rasputin.

The proceedings were disrupted by the arrival of two limousines to my right, from which emerged Gavin Smart and a gaggle of what could only have been attorneys. Shouts of "there he is" accompanied the reorientation and scramble of the mass of humanity in Smart's direction, like an amoeba extending an arm of protoplasm in response to an enticing stimulus, then rapidly pulling the rest of itself towards it.

In a flash, a new impromptu press conference organized itself. Smart's lead attorney began holding forth. From my vantage point above the action, I noticed an elderly woman, hobbling along with a cane, approach the new arrivals. Alone, she slowly crossed in front of me, behind Gavin Smart and his legal team.

As she reached a point directly behind Smart, a few steps up, she stopped, as if to catch her breath. She reached into her handbag, took out what appeared to be a knitting needle, and lunged at Smart. She weighed barely 100 pounds, and had little muscle left on her frail frame, but she was falling down the steps, and all it took was aim; gravity did the rest. She buried the needle in the back of Gavin Smart's neck.

* * *

She told the police she had come across the country to help her son, but, when she arrived at the jail, she discovered she was too late. All she could do was identify his body.

She had done that first thing in the morning, then took a taxi to the courthouse to see the monster the Internet said had killed her son. Then things just sort of happened.

Gavin Smart lingered in a vegetative state for weeks until the plug was finally pulled.

Even Dargo had a mother.

Chapter 59

I met FBI Special Agent in Charge Alex Greene at Vasona Park, just a few miles south of my office. He had chosen the location, probably to be away from his staff and assure we weren't overheard. It was very cloak-and-dagger.

We sat on a bench, soaking up the sun, far from the playgrounds and picnic areas, with a great view of the lake. Ducks were paddling. Parents and kids were paddle boating. Canadian Geese were waddling around the acres of open parkland, pooping,

Greene wore a red golf shirt, tan Dockers and brown loafers. He had on dark, wrap-around sunglasses. I figured this was his casual disguise.

He took some sort of ShushNik-sized device out of his pocket and waved it at me. "Jams all electronic devices within 50 feet," he said. "It's on." He put the jammer back in his pocket. I fought to keep my amusement in check.

"Okay, Joe, what's this about Venezuela?"

When I called Greene's office and spoke to his admin, I asked her to have him call me.

"What is this concerning?" she had dutifully asked.

"Venezuela."

"That's it?"

"That's it. He'll understand."

He had.

"Here's what bothered me," I said. "You told me all that stuff about triangular trade and Varga's role in the money laundering scheme, including details of the raid on the warehouse where Isidora stupidly left the pallets as evidence of the diamond smuggling. I'm sort of green at this, but there's no way the FBI is so forthcoming with a guy like me, no matter how well you know the folks at Kowalski-Wu. You are legendary for revealing the least possible amount of information."

Greene was inscrutable behind his sunglasses, nearly motionless.

"Then there was the way Navarro Varga travelled, with just one or two bodyguards and a single vehicle. I think a guy who launders money for several Mexican cartels would have a larger entourage. Especially when we went to Gilroy, I can't imagine him not having a fleet of vehicles and an army of thugs with him. In fact, I would have expected him to send his gang to fetch Isidora and bring her to him, while he waited somewhere he had ample security.

"As for detecting Conflict Diamonds and backtracking them from the San Francisco diamond district to the Pottery Mexico Warehouse, my research says you can't. International agreements about diamond certification and tracking have been mainly for show.

"I did see news reports about the FBI breaking up a ring that smuggled drug cash out of the United States to Mexico and shipped it to Africa to exchange for Conflict Diamonds bound for cartel agents in Brazil. The president even took credit for it in a tweet. But my hunch is, that was going on anyway and had nothing to do with Varga. It was a good move to build that part of your story to me on a real, unrelated investigation."

The corners of Greene's mouth twitched slightly, as if he were suppressing a smile. Or a snarl.

"You said the DEA had been all over Varga and his shipments but they found nothing. I know they use x-ray equipment and they would certainly have x-rayed the clay pots. They're not complete bozos. Would they have overlooked the pallets? I don't think so. Wouldn't the diamonds have shown up on those x-rays?"

Greene sat sunning himself, like an ebony sphynx.

"Here's what I think. There were diamonds, but Varga was smuggling them out of the country, not in. They were first smuggled into California by Venezuelan mobsters, who themselves were brought in illegally by another part of Varga's organization. Not your ordinary coyotes herding poor Latinos across the border. It was an upscale, comfortable travel service for well-heeled Venezuelans and their families. The very government officials and their cronies who had been looting their country for years and were now heading here, much like the communist crooks came here after the fall of the Soviet Union. Just what we need, a new Venezuelan Mafia in America.

"They came in small groups. It might take several trips for a whole family. They paid well from part of the stash of diamonds they brought with them. These were sophisticated crooks, they only paid for each person after they were safely at their Northern California destination.

"Then Pottery Mexico would bake those payments, now Varga's diamonds, into a clay pot in the San Jose warehouse. They'd break up the pot and smuggle the diamonds into

Mexico in plain view. They were inside some shards, just broken rejects, in the back of a truck innocently returning across the border from its delivery of pots up north.

"Isidora Ramirez ran that for Varga. After the bad personal business with Jesus, she had stolen Navarro's last batch of diamonds and split. After I met with you the first time, you found her and convinced her to entrap Varga. Then she took over the Venezuelan operation and helped you bust it. All that stuff about her doing a runner after the Gilroy thing was my imagination running wild. I bought your fairy tale and thought I was the clever one. You and Agent Kwon went along with my fantasy and played me for a sucker."

Greene finally broke his silence. "Sucker seems a bit harsh. Let's say your wild tale has some truth to it. How did you figure it out?"

"Remember when you said the United States wasn't nearly as concerned about people smuggling things out of the country as into it? That got me thinking. Then I saw the *Mercury News* series about the FBI busting the Venezuelan people smuggling operation, sending the crooks who had looted Venezuela home to justice. They didn't have all the details, but there were enough for me to piece it together. And your picture in the paper announcing the bust was a helpful clue."

"I can't confirm any of this," Greene said.

"No need. I'll keep my mouth shut." But FBI Special Agent in Charge Alex Greene would owe me a favor.

* * *

I decided to let Greene think I had the deductive powers of Sherlock Holmes. What I left out was the thing that had really put the whole story together for me. It was a letter I received in the mail, hand printed on lined paper, postmarked Fresno, California. It was from someone to whom I had given my business card not too long ago.

Dear Joe,

My class is learning about friendly letters. I need to send a letter to a friend.

Diego and I go to a nice school. We live in a nice house with a nice lady named Maria.

Mommy is away in a place called Caracas. She is working for a green man. Isn't that funny? She says she will be home soon. She said the green man will give her one of his colored cards that she needs.

Thank you for being my friend and my hero.

Sincerely,
Sofia

P.S. My teacher helped us with spelling and mailing.

Chapter 60

Living at home with your parents does not make for a good sex life. Especially when your new girlfriend, which Anna had become, lives at home with her parents. And each of the houses is small, with all the bedrooms and the bathroom off one hall. Not much privacy conducive to romance.

And so it was that I had decided to take the big step of getting my own place. I had just invested my unexpectedly big payoff from solving the Perfect Murder.

Ryan had given me a fat bonus for solving that case and rescuing his mother from Rex's murderer. I mean fat as in six figures. Ridiculous, I know, but who was I to argue? This bonanza was followed by a six-figure advance from a Hollywood production company for the exclusive rights to my take on the Perfect Murder story.

After talking to Nick Marchetti, the only financial guru I happen to know, I decided to use most of my windfall for a down payment on a new condo in a complex just a couple of miles from my office. It was Nick's advice. I was socking away the money where I wouldn't be tempted to fritter it away, in a good, long-term investment, and taking advantage of historically low interest rates to get a fixed-rate mortgage I could afford.

Afford? Hah! It wasn't like I got a paycheck I could count

on. One thing I had learned since I became self-employed was that meeting monthly commitments helps focus your mind on income. You know, the opposite of outgo.

Anyway, I was finally going to be out of the family home. All grown up and independent. Adulting like crazy, as my friends say. And it wasn't just the privacy issue. Age 30 was not far off. It was time.

I had just returned from signing all the paperwork at the title company, thinking about generating income to pay all my new bills, when Boomer walked into my office.

"You look awfully happy, young fella," he said.

I told Boomer my news and he congratulated me.

"Your day in the Valley?"

"That, and I need your help with something."

Another day, another case. Hopefully, one that paid.

Acknowledgements

Thanks once again to my editors. To my wife, Lois, who helps me get the plot and characters to the finish line together. To my sister-in-law, Judy, whose proofreading is beyond compare. I could not turn my writing into a novel without both of you.

I also want to thank readers who take the time to write a review on Amazon. I love the feedback, and others appreciate your thoughts.

About the Author

Phil Bookman had a long career as a software entrepreneur, starting a number of successful software companies. He is now retired from the software industry, and spends much of his time writing mystery novels with Silicon Valley heroes.

Phil grew up in Seaford, New York, where he met and married his high school sweetheart, Lois. He has degrees from Rensselaer Polytechnic Institute, Adelphi University and Santa Clara University. Lois and Phil reside in Los Gatos, California and have lived in Silicon Valley since 1974.

Contact Phil at philtheauthor@outlook.com
Visit Phil's author page at philbookman.com
All Phil's books are available on Amazon.com

Also by Phil Bookman

Fiction

Mike Gold Mystery Series

Santa's Village (Book 10)

Gold Moonshot (Book 9)

The Yippee Murders (Book 8)

Gold Jihad (Book 7)

Death Order (Book 6)

Alias (Book 5)

Slice (Book 4)

Riding the Tiger (Book 3)

Charisma (Book 2)

Opium (Book 1)

Non-Fiction

Attacking The Crown Jewels

Made in the USA
Middletown, DE
07 November 2023

42129888R00168